THE HOUR OF THE FOX

ALSO BY KURT PALKA

Rosegarden
The Chaperon
Equinox
Scorpio Moon
Clara (originally published as Patient Number 7)
The Piano Maker

The

HOUR

of the

FOX

A Novel

KURT PALKA

McClelland & Stewart

Library and Archives Canada Cataloguing in Publication is available upon request

ISBN: 978-0-7710-7381-6
ebook ISBN: 978-0-7710-7382-3

Typeset in Perpetua by M&S, Toronto
Book design by Rachel Cooper
Cover art: © Stas Pushkarev / Arcangel
Printed and bound in the USA

McClelland & Stewart,
a division of Penguin Random House Canada Limited,
a Penguin Random House Company
www.penguinrandomhouse.ca

1 2 3 4 5   22 21 20 19 18

Penguin
Random House
McCLELLAND & STEWART

For Heather
and for Christina and Paul, and Melanie and Rob

She followed slowly, taking a long time,
as though there were something she had yet to overcome,
but also as if, as soon as she had done so,
she might no longer merely walk, but fly.

RAINER MARIA RILKE, *New Poems* (1907)

CONTENTS

DOWN HERE,
AMONG HUMANS

One

THE HOUSE WAS DARK, as she'd known it would be. She thought he was in South America, but she was not certain. In Argentina, maybe.

She unlatched the garden gate and walked down the path, around the main house and down to the cottage, past the roses and the quince bushes all in darkness but the concrete path brighter than the grass and the earth around it. At the cottage she unlocked the door and went in.

She put her briefcase on the counter, and for a moment it looked to her as though a light had come on and gone out again in one of the windows at the main house. She watched a while longer to see if the light came back but it didn't. The house still dark, a brick mountain looming in the night. Then a light flashed again, but now she could tell that it was only the reflection of the headlights of a car going by in the street. It wasn't Jack.

She hesitated for a moment, then took the key from her purse and walked back up the path to the house. The bushes were full of their fruit that no one picked any more. When Andrew had been small, they used to make quince jelly together, the boy helping her pick and mash, and later in the coldroom in the basement taking the jars from her hand and setting them on the low shelf with the labels pointing front. In later years an English neighbour came to pick some of the fruit, but that ended too.

She unlocked the back door, pushed it open and listened, then reached for the light switch and stepped inside. Cold, damp. Stairway air. Up she walked, feeling like an intruder, turning on lights as she went: the hallway; the kitchen, all modern and unused like a showroom; the TV room; the living room; her study with the door closed; his study with the door open. She paused for a moment, then stepped inside.

Bookcases, his desk, tray after tray with his rock samples. On two large corkboards maps full of pins with little flags for copper, gold, and silver, all the treasures of the earth. And prominently on the keyboard of his upright typewriter, the thing she'd been hoping for, a sheet of paper with his handwriting on it: *Argentina, Río Negro, Aguada de*

Guerra. And a telephone number. She took the piece of paper, folded it, and put it in her pocket. Over at the southern hemisphere map, she looked for Argentina and Río Negro. There. A little pin with a silver flag in Aguada de Guerra.

At the door she looked back into the room that was so completely filled with him. For a moment her vision shimmered, and she pressed a finger to her eyebrow. Not now, she said to it. Not now.

That night she slept on the couch in the living room at the main house. She got ready in the bathroom, and then in their bedroom gathered pillow and duvet off the bed and dragged them into the living room. She found a night-gown and put it on and crawled into the nest. Light from passing cars brushing the ceiling. Once in the night she thought she heard the telephone and she stumbled to it thinking it might be Andrew, but there was only the dial tone and the receiver cold and heavy in her hand.

Later in a dream she saw him on a canvas stretcher in the desert, and she was his nurse to make him well again. Except that she could only occasionally glance at him through the heat-shimmer before she had to go back to counting grains of sand from one hand into the other. So many grains of sand. When she finally walked over to the stretcher she had exactly the same number of grains in each hand, and that seemed important. She meant to tell him, but he was gone and there was only the empty stretcher.

"Dear Margaret," Aileen had said to her not that long ago. "He was a good boy and he knew what he wanted and that's exactly what he did. Stop questioning him and yourself. Let him go. He would want you to."

They'd been sitting in Aileen's living room in Sweetbarry and the sun was going down red, red on Gull Rock out there, and red upon the tips of the tallest trees in her father's little forest, the cedars and the pines.

She and Aileen had been friends and neighbours in Sweetbarry all their lives, and that long weekend she'd flown there simply for Aileen's strength and kindness and for help with her own thinking, which was like wandering a dark maze with no way out.

It had been several months after Andrew had been killed and his coffin had come home empty, and eventually she had told Jack face to face that she was hoping he'd understand, and that she believed she still loved him, but that she could not live with him right now. Rather than increase her strength, being with him actually weakened and distracted her. From this, she said. From what she needed to learn to do now. From finding her way back to herself. If it was all right with him, she would be moving out of the main house for a while, into the little wooden cottage at the bottom of the garden to be alone.

This had been one morning in the hallway, in the light from the open bathroom door. Jack had stood looking at her, so very careful with her now.

"The cottage," he'd said. "Really? I don't know what condition it's in, Margaret. As you know, Andrew and his friends used it off and on but nobody has really lived in it for years. Are you sure?"

"I'm sure, Jack."

The place did need repairs, and she decided to take care of those herself. She queried the men at the lumber-yard in great detail about what she would need and how to do it, and she made lists and bought tools and sup-plies, and got on with it: new flooring in two areas in the kitchen and bedroom where the boards were rotten, repairs to plaster where it had come away from laths, repairs to the siding on the south wall, and new roofing shingles in several places.

Altogether the repairs took five weekends. On the last weekend Jack was home, and he watched from the kitchen window and at times from the walkway. She was up on the roof, fitting and hammering, and while getting up there had been relatively easy, coming back down was not. Jack didn't say anything, asked no questions and knew better than to offer help. But he brought down two electric heaters from the main house and set them on the path not far from the cottage. She would have liked to smile at him but she feared it might make her weep, which she didn't want to do any more, and so she did not smile. He stood for some time, then he turned and walked back up to the house and stepped inside and closed the door.

In the morning she tidied couch and bedroom and put everything back exactly the way it had been. The night-gown she refolded along its creases and put it back in the same spot in the same drawer in the dresser. Like a thief she tiptoed from room to room making sure there were no traces of her having nested there the night. In the hallway she picked up the receiver and listened and put it down again.

She went to work by subway as usual, and in her office she closed the door, unfolded Jack's note and smoothed it on her desk. She took a deep breath and let it out and then dialled the number and asked for Señor Jack Bradley. Her Spanish was good enough for her to understand that the girl was asking for her name and number so that Señor Bradley could call her back.

When he called, Jenny was in the room taking dictation for the meeting with the Chicago client that evening, and Margaret asked her to come back in fifteen minutes and close the door on the way out.

"Is everything all right?" he said.

"More or less. I have a question. Where was Andrew on that last mission? I know it was in Ethiopia, but was it in a hot and sandy place?"

There was a silence on the phone, and even across these thousands of miles of wire she could feel him shifting down into his careful mode.

"You want to do this all over again? It won't change with the retelling."

"Just tell me if it was hot and sandy."

"Probably. In places, anyway. There are highlands and there's the Ahmar mountain range but that's a bit further north. South in the Ogaden region, where he was, there'd be some vegetation but there'd also be stretches of desert."

"On an airstrip."

"Yes, on an improvised airstrip. You know that."

"He wanted to be like you," she said.

"Like me. Are we back to that now? He wanted to be like me and so it's my influence on him, again. Or the lack of it. I never wanted to be a pilot or a soldier. Not after I saw how the war messed up my father. I wanted him to become an engineer, and he made a good start at it. He got his first degree and could have gone on, but then he discovered flying. Why are you doing this again? I thought we were done with the blaming."

"I'm not *blaming* you. But you know he admired you and wanted to be like you. The military history in your family."

"No, I don't know that. Not after what my father did."

More silence on the phone then.

"Wait," she said quickly. "Jack . . . I don't mean to . . ."

And he did wait a while, but when she took too long he said, "Take care, Margaret. I'll probably be home on Monday. We need to talk." And he hung up.

Two

IN THE AFTERNOON she and Hugh Templeton had a short meeting about the Chicago case, a 120-million-dollar acquisition and repositioning of a Canadian company by an American client. She had written the two-page executive summary, and Hugh read it and they discussed the main points.

"You'll be the lead," he said to her then. "You talk them through it. All right?"

Hugh was the senior partner in the law firm, and she worked closely with him. Altogether there were four partners and seven associates, including her. She was the most senior associate, and the understanding was that as long as she kept performing as well as she had been, she was next in line to make partner.

To accommodate the client's schedule, the boardroom meeting took place after regular office hours. She and Hugh sat side by side, across the table from the client and his lawyer and his accountant. For several minutes while the men sat reading the summary, there was not one sound in the room save for the occasional creaking of a chair. The overhead lights were on, and out the window she could see that the sky was darkening. There had been rain in the forecast. In some of the buildings lights were coming on.

"And this?" the client's lawyer said. He was a big man in a pinstripe suit, and he had pale eyes that stared at her with the same mocking condescension that she used to get from men as a student and as a young woman lawyer but that she hadn't seen in a long time. He turned the page her way with his broad finger on a paragraph. "This part, ma'am." Not even bothering with her name.

But she knew by now how to deal with men like him. She'd learned it in law school and in all the years thereafter, in job after job, and now she gave him her unhurried look, steady and calm, waiting for him to see himself in her eyes, and within a few heartbeats he did. The response was always the same, and it flickered from surprise to embarrassment, and something in his face and even in the way he held his shoulders changed.

"Offshore residency, Ted," she said. "Is that not clear? It's set up that way in point three. See? And there's more detail a few lines down."

She turned away from him to the client and explained briefly about offshore registration and how, when a corporation bought into Canada through the back door in this way, the tax advantage was actually threefold.

Jenny brought a tray with deli sandwiches and carafes and cups and napkins. She glanced questioningly at Margaret, and Margaret checked her watch and nodded.

The men went back to reading.

Out the window against the sky she saw a flight of pigeons circling. They fluttered and then landed on the windowsills of the bank building at the King Street corner.

The first raindrops tapped against the glass, and abruptly, before the rain became too heavy, she pushed back her chair and stood up and walked there and opened the door for air.

It was an old-fashioned glass-paned double door leading to the shallow ledge of a French balcony enclosed by an ironwork railing. For a long moment she stood there in her business suit and the black heels that pinched her toes, and out of nowhere the smell of rain on warm masonry reminded her of her youth, of her student days so long ago, the ruined postwar streets of Paris and the excitement of a new place so filled with defiance and ideas.

Down in the street, car roofs glistened and people under umbrellas crowded the subway entrance. Car headlights were coming on, rain in the beams of light. A young black dog suddenly darted off the sidewalk and into traffic, where it bumped against a car. The dog rolled and yelped and then stood in confusion. One car nearly rear-ended another and drivers honked their horns and a woman stood and screamed the dog's name.

For a moment her vision shimmered and her heart pounded and none of what she saw made sense to her. And yet it did, in some lifetime arc wanting completion, standing at that glass wall again at Lakewood, all so long ago. And now this, all this, with her mind free to roam among losses and dangers, and free to see and connect the now with the then, and the young dog and the woman in the wet street, and this feeling again of not being who she thought she was. Of having slipped her mooring and being adrift between worlds.

Down in the street the dog found its owner, a woman perhaps her own age who crouched with her coattails on the wet sidewalk and hugged the dog and struggled to snap a leash to its collar. It was a black lab, an over-joyed puppy thrashing its tail, licking the woman's face and hands, and all the while Margaret stood with her right hand on the iron rail and the fingertips of her left to her eyebrow. She must not let the men see her like this . . .

"Margaret," said Hugh Templeton behind her back. "*Margaret?* We're ready here."

She took a deep breath and closed the door and returned to the table. Walking there she concentrated on the way the shoes pinched her toes, on the very pinpoints of pain, to focus her mind. She allowed her feet to slide forward as far as they would go, pushed them hard into the narrow toe box. Zach at the clinic had taught her about that.

Back in her chair she took charge, taking them step by step through the transaction and all the alternatives and consequences. As she talked, it became easier. It always did. She was back in the lifeboat of her profession now, where she felt strong and in control. This was her métier, and with perseverance and hard work over the years she had made herself one of the best in it.

The client and his lawyer picked up on the change in the room and they sat forward and began making notes.

When she was done she took off her reading glasses, folded them, and put them on the table.

"Gentlemen. Any questions?"

They looked at each other, nodded at each other to speak first. There were no questions, the client said, but there was a lot to think about.

Such as? They raised a few points, and she jotted them down, considered them, then went over them in detail.

In the end they asked for a draft agreement to be sent to their Chicago office. And in a few days' time perhaps a telephone conference, the client said.

It had gotten late.

Hugh, relieved and chatty, walked them to the elevator. And she, alone in the boardroom now, opened the balcony door again and inhaled the sweet air. The rain had stopped. Night out there.

Thank you, she said.

Much later, in the kitchen at the cottage, she picked at a TV dinner and glanced up at the main house, all in darkness. She stepped outside into the cool night, all those bushes and trees washed clean. She took a few deep breaths, looked up at the sky and up at the house again, and turned back into the kitchen.

Near eleven she called Michael at home. She sat on the bed, in her robe with her face scrubbed and her hair down. She had her knees pulled up and at times she talked resting her forehead on them.

Into one of her pauses he said, "Margaret? Will you be all right there tonight? In that cabin? Why not go up to the main house again?"

"It's not that bad in here, Michael. It's actually quite nice."

"What's the name of the all-night drugstore on Yonge Street near you? I'll call in a prescription."

"No, I don't want anything. Most of that stuff turns me into a zombie, but I need to be able to function. And I'm able to, during the day. The nights are something else."

"There's a new antidepressant we can try. We could start with a low dose."

"No, Michael. Listen, I called Jack."

"And?"

"And nothing. It didn't go well."

"What happened?"

"The usual."

After a silence Michael said, "Please try to remember that pharmacy name. I can look up the phone number. Have you used the codeine?"

"Once or twice. I don't like the side effects of that either, but I'm keeping one ready in my pocket."

With her forehead off her knees now she said, "I had another dream about having been too busy. Lately I keep thinking I let Andrew down. Neglected him when he was small and I was working all the time. I often worked until one and two in the morning and Jack was never there."

"Not *never*."

"He was gone much more than he was home. Not that I ever complained, because from the beginning we had a deal, a career for both of us. I was home for the first eight months with Andrew, but then I hired nannies and started looking for work."

"Many women do that."

"These days, maybe. Not then. Sometimes when it got late and I couldn't leave the office, I'd pump breast milk in the washroom and send it home to the nanny in a taxi. One time a young lawyer found out and from then on the joke was, *I'll have full-fat in mine, Mags.* They called me the Milkmaid behind my back. But I was determined to hang in, Michael. So determined. Only now when I think back, I'm asking myself if maybe with all the focus on work I let my boy down."

There was a pause, and she always liked him for that, for the space he gave her.

"I don't think you let Andrew down," he said eventually. "Margaret, please listen. Andrew's death is not your fault. It is not your fault. What you are going through now is a common second-stage response. Since there is no one else to blame, we tend to look for the cause within ourselves. But when Andrew boarded that plane, he was a grown young man and he did what he'd signed up for. What he wanted to do."

"But maybe I hadn't equipped him to make the right choices. And why do I want to remember him more as a little boy than as a grown man? Learning to ride a bicycle, and all those baseball practices that I drove him to and picked him up from. His thrilled excitement when he'd done well. His fresh-air boy-smell next to me in the car. So healthy, Michael. So very much alive and with so much to look forward to, to try out and explore. And then school and university and the training, and when that bus took him away it felt like just a short time later, and I didn't realize he was actually *leaving*. And how could I have known? How could he? It's all so unfinished."

"I know. I do know, Margaret."

"And then he never did come home again."

"I know, Margaret. I understand."

She was weeping now and couldn't help it. It was all wrong, all askew, and she didn't know how to make it straight again.

"Margaret? Never mind about that drugstore. I can call information. I think it's a Guardian something. I'll come and see you on the weekend. Let's say Sunday mid-afternoon. Will that be all right?"

"And Lakewood," she said to him. "Even that's come back. I didn't want it to, but today at the office window it did."

"We've dealt with Lakewood, Margaret. More than once. It's in a safe place, so let's leave it alone for now."

She said okay, okay, and he asked again if Sunday mid-afternoon would be all right, and she said yes.

That same night, at one o'clock in the morning and then again at two and at three, she looked up toward the main house and wished there were lights on in the windows. Not so dark, not so looming. And then she was glad there weren't any lights, because they would mean she'd have to face Jack, when she had quite forgotten how to do that in good faith. It was hard enough on the phone, and it would be worse face to face. What to say, how to be with him, who not so long ago had been her everything and she could wrap herself in him as in a garment and feel loved and be her true self. That was what she'd lost, the wellspring of that ability within herself. That and the humour and the fine intelligence between them. And had replaced it with what? With guilt and confusion and a flow of memories about past events and Andrew. With all that to be dealt with.

In the kitchen of this cottage that she'd fixed up herself like a hiding place in the woods, she'd found refuge, and it was here that for some reason she could talk with Andrew, always with the boy he'd been, when he'd still listened. When he'd still looked up and watched her face so earnestly, watched her expression.

And she imagined he could hear when in whispers as soft as thoughts she talked to him about the poison that in recent weeks was eating her. The idea, so common after the war and well into the 1950s and even the '60s, that women in selfish pursuit of a profession always let their children down. Too busy. Scorned by the full-time mothers and dedicated homemakers doing it right.

But when he'd been small, had she ever felt she was letting him down? Not laying the right foundation? If she was honest, hardly ever. Perhaps in weak moments, as an excuse to abandon her own struggles. Abandon her dream of a career, of who she wanted to become. When first Lakewood, then Paris, then law school, and finally Jack had helped her to see that so very clearly.

At Lakewood they hadn't been allowed in the dormitory in daytime, but on weekends when the matron and half the staff were off, Sister Elvira would let them in for an hour in the afternoon. It was a golden fall, and the girls, all in different stages of pregnancy, would crowd the row of windows to watch the boats going by on Lake Rosseau, the fine wooden Muskoka launches burbling past, each carrying women in white dresses under a green canvas fly roof sipping from champagne glasses and eating small sandwiches off a tray, and the men in the cockpit dressed in white as well, passing a flask and wiping their lips on the backs of their hands. And always the men would look up and see the girls at the windows, and then the men would lean close to say something their women couldn't hear, but the girls could see their lips moving and their eyes looking up, and the boat would glide on, smooth and luxurious, just a breath of smoke lifting off the water behind it and hardly a wake at all to show its passing.

In her own time there, her six months of 1946–47, not one of the girls was older than seventeen. She herself was just sixteen and a half.

One of the girls, a fifteen-year-old from New York, had a pair of opera glasses, and through them they would pick out loving parents for their children: rich, elegant men and kind women in white. This one, they'd exclaim. Or that one, the one with the blond curly hair and the shirt sleeves rolled up. He looks nice! And excitedly they'd pass the glasses up and down the line of girls, some of them going on eight and nine months, some just four or five.

She heated some milk on the stove and poured it into a cup and then stepped outside into the cool air and sipped the steaming liquid. Some stars tonight, a few moonlit clouds. She looked up at the house, the windows all dark. He'd be home on Monday, he'd said. He wanted to talk, and she was not looking forward to it.

Eventually she stepped back inside and washed out the cup and saucepan and put them on the drain rack. She left the little light on in the kitchen and went to bed.

Three

SOMETIME IN THE WEEKS before Lakewood there had been the night when she heard them talking at a near whisper, Father and Grandmother AJ, down in the living room at Sweetbarry while she was sitting at the top of the stairs.

"For her own good—you understand that, Charles, don't you? Look at me. For the girl's own good. So she made a mistake, but down here, among humans, that's what we do. We make mistakes. This one you might as well blame on her youth and on her innocent bloom and on that boy, and on nature's relentless push toward the only thing that matters to it. More babies, more trees, more rabbits, just blindly more of everything. She says she felt pressured and was tempted and was confused, and so forth. It's the same sad old story repeated a million times over. But we don't want her to have to pay for that one mistake forever. Right, Charles? Say something."

But he said nothing, or perhaps he just nodded, and Grandmother continued.

"I've spoken to the boy's father. Not an easy conversation, as you can imagine. Twice, in fact, and now it's all arranged. No one around here will ever know, and the less said the better."

"Who's the boy?"

"A summer boy. A blond sixteen-year-old kid from Montreal. A nice kid, except for this now. You've seen him around. They always rent the house with the green shutters on the other side of town."

For a while there was silence down there, and Margaret strained to hear.

"I'm actually proud of her, Charles," Grandmother said. "It must have taken a lot of courage for her to come and ask for my help. Most girls wouldn't. They'd just stand on the train track and stare at the light coming."

"What's his name?"

"His name. Unless you really want to know and get involved, don't even ask. Maybe just let me deal with it. I've put a lot of work into it already. Lakewood will be perfect for her. They even have a schoolroom and tutors up there, and doctors, of course. She'll probably fall a bit behind with her studies, but I've spoken to Thérèse in Paris, and that is exactly what her school is set up for. To help girls in situations like this catch up. Margaret can do her baccalaureate there and then go on to university and law school. Put all this behind her and get a profession. A solid career. That's what I would have wanted for myself."

"As though nothing ever happened?" said Father. "You really believe that these things leave no marks?"

"Of course they do. For a while. But what are the alternatives, Charles? Tell me."

Grandmother, always so clear and strong. Until that night she'd often feared her, sometimes even hated her. This, not that, Margaret. Pay attention. Think for yourself, child, always.

For a while there was silence down there again. Then Grandmother said, "Exactly. Our Margaret is young and bright and she has a future. Let's not have her waste it. I'll talk to her again tomorrow, but I wanted you to know. Don't make that face, Charles. Do you agree with the plan?"

"Do I have a choice?"

"Of course you do. Tell me."

Through all this she sat hugging her knees on the landing, feeling new waves of gratitude and respect for Grandmother. It was late, past midnight. She'd gone to the bathroom and on her way back to bed had heard her name.

"Charles?" Grandmother was saying down there again. "Do you agree?"

Next day when they were alone in the house, Grandmother sat her down at the oak table in the kitchen and told her in more detail what the plans were. Lakewood was a retreat and a clinic and an adoption centre all at once.

"It's unfortunate what happened, Margaret, but it's not the end of the world. I've spoken to Xavier's father, and he was shocked of course, and angry, but in the end he agreed to the Lakewood plan. He would not agree to anything else, such as long-term obligations if on some misguided notion you should want to keep and raise the baby. He'll pay for half of Lakewood, and he'll even contribute to the private school in Paris so you can catch up. I was quite firm with him."

"They've packed up already and gone back to Montreal," she said. "There was even a truck that took away bits of furniture. I saw it from the post office."

"Did you now. It's easy for boys, isn't it? Look at me, Margaret. All this will pass. We'll work it out. I promise."

But she couldn't look at Grandmother. She sat kneading her fingers, thinking how confused and embarrassed she was. How angry.

"The school in Paris is called École Olivier," said Grandmother. "A distant relative of ours runs it. Thérèse Lafontaine. She's the cousin of a niece of mine. I've spoken to her already. What happened doesn't make you a bad person, Margaret, but it does make you vulnerable. I suggest you tell no one. Aileen, perhaps, if you really must. Any gossip about it will attach to you forever in this community, and that's not what you want. Trust me about this. If your mother were here with us today, she would advise you to do the same. Margaret, please look at me."

She finally looked up from her hands and across the table at Grandmother.

"You need to put all this behind you, dear. Start again and make something of yourself. First things first. Become good at something, and then organize your life around that gift. Get a career, a vision. A foundation for yourself that no one can take away, and *then* have your children, as many as you want and can afford. It's all possible, Margaret. You'll see."

That afternoon she and Aileen took the rowboat out to Gull Rock and they sat with their brown legs in the water, on their spot on the rock where it was smooth and flat and shaped just right. Both in their bathing suits, the bottoms worn thin on these sun-warm rocks with the little mosses and tiny purple flowers that smelled of honey if you put your nose right to them.

They stuck out their legs and kicked them up and down, playing motorboat to see who could go faster.

They laughed and stopped kicking.

"Shift over a bit," said Aileen. "So I can see the house in case Mom's waving for me to come in."

Margaret shifted. She said, "Did you hand in the application?"

"I did. Yesterday. They told me more or less what to expect. Turns out it'll take years. Years." Aileen lay back on the rock.

"Not that many. Four, five? How long do you think it'll take me with the law school bit? If I can even get in."

"You'll get in," said Aileen. She sat up again. "They told me that while I'm candy-striping I'll need to take a bunch of courses. Well, I knew that. Six of them, can you believe it? And there'll be exams at different levels. But if everything goes well I could be a nurse in training, a real NIT, by the time I'm nineteen. Then more courses and the licensing bit, and a couple of years later I could be a real nurse."

For a while they said nothing, and all they could hear was the ocean and a few gulls somewhere.

"Aileen," she said then. "If I tell you a deep, deep, a very deep secret, will you look at me and we cross fingers and you swear to me that you'll never tell anyone? No one, ever? Will you?"

Aileen sat very still suddenly.

"Will you?"

"You sure, Margaret?"

"I am, if you promise. I want you to know. I need you to know. And I trust you. It'll help me."

"All right, I promise."

And solemnly they both held out the fore and middle fingers of their right hands and crossed them.

A week or two later, on the last day before they turned off the water and closed up the house in Sweetbarry to move back to Toronto, she stood naked in front of the mirror and looked at herself. Because she had always been so slim, she thought she could already see the baby showing. She wondered if Aileen had already known when they were sitting on Gull Rock that time. Noticed something but didn't say anything, and like a true friend did not probe but waited and hoped to be told. That would be like Aileen.

———

At Lakewood there was the little clinic and a nursery and a recovery room behind white swing doors, and there were the schoolroom and the kitchen and dining and other rooms in the basement, and the dormitory facing the lake. The one area that was absolutely off limits to them was the entrance and the gravel drive in front of the building. And because they weren't allowed even to be seen in any of the windows above the entrance, they had to imagine what went on there, and they discussed it in colourful detail.

They imagined fine chauffeur-driven cars pulling up and men and women in elegant clothes climbing out, and the matron welcoming them and then leading the way to her office. And perhaps an hour later, with papers having been signed and the transaction concluded, the new parents would come back out and walk to their car, and the chauffeur would open the door for the woman, who was holding a newborn in a little blanket, kissing its tiny face and cooing at it and having absolutely no eyes for anything else.

From those imaginary people and from the real people in the boats going by they chose the parents for their children. The woman Margaret finally selected had a kind face and a lovely smile, and the man was the one with the blond curly hair they'd seen in the mahogany boat, the one with the sleeves rolled up on strong arms. On the day when they'd come to Lakewood to take home her baby, he would be wearing a white linen jacket and the woman a white dress, and she would look happy with her arm in his. Margaret could clearly see his firm step and the kindness in the woman's face, and that was enough for her.

During Margaret's time at Lakewood, Aileen came to visit her twice, once in late October and the second time during Christmas. It was a long journey for her, from Halifax by train to Montreal with a nighttime wait and change of trains, and then on to Toronto and north from there with Father and Grandmother in the car. Margaret offered to pay for the train tickets from her allowance, but Aileen would agree only to a fifty-fifty split.

At Lakewood there was a visiting room in the basement, but there were usually other parents and girls present. People whispered and there was no privacy. And so on both visits she and Aileen snuck out the back door and propped it open, and they hugged, and at first Margaret was teary-eyed because it was so good to see Aileen.

In October Aileen told her that the house with the green shutters had been rented full-time now, and it seemed that Xavier's family would not be back for the summers. Margaret listened. She looked away from Aileen and down at the ground, and after a while she looked up and said it did not matter.

She told Aileen about the boats going by and how they were choosing parents, and how that might seem imaginary but it helped them and so in some way it was also real.

And she talked about day-to-day life at Lakewood and how here, unlike at St. Gregory's, the high school where she'd been in Toronto, there was real camaraderie and mutual support among the girls. Perhaps the closeness of survivorship, she said.

She could laugh about that, here among the flaming bushes in the fresh air with Aileen. Aileen in her cords and running shoes and a windbreaker, with her black hair blowing and her clear eyes so attentive. Margaret described how sometimes in the night, when one of the new girls could be heard sobbing in the dark, the eight- or nine-monther whose turn it was that week would pad barefoot over there and sit in silence on the edge of the girl's bed for company. It was something they'd come up with and worked out among themselves.

By the time of her Christmas visit, Aileen was already candy-striping part-time at the hospital. She described her duties at length, and as she did so her face was flushed with excitement. Margaret had rarely seen her so happy, and it made her happy too.

"I think I might actually manage to do it," Aileen said. "Get to be a real nurse someday. Can you believe it, Margaret? It's so amazing. A real nurse!"

Both times when she came to visit, Aileen managed to smuggle in a bag of chocolate chip cookies, which the girls shared the same night, sitting on their bunks and nibbling away like kittens. The telltale cookie bags she'd crumple up and sneak them out to the incinerator and watch them flare up in the dark.

Four

ON SUNDAY AFTERNOON she watched Michael
from the cottage window as he walked along the path.
He had on a grey vested suit and a burgundy bowtie,
and he was carrying his scuffed brown doctor bag. When
he arrived she met him in the doorway.

"This is nicer than I thought," he said. "No one would
guess it from the street. And smack in the middle of
Rosedale."

"You've never been down here? In all these years?"

"Never. I've seen the roof through the trees from the
main house, and I know some of the story with Jack's
father. But I've never been in it."

"Jack's grandfather had it built. Colonel Bradley, after
his wife died and he wanted to be alone. Jack says they
were a wonderful love story. He says his grandfather was

everything that his father was not. Especially after the war."

She led him through the kitchen into the living room, where one window gave a view toward the ravine and the other showed the main house, behind trees perhaps thirty yards uphill.

"And you fixed it up yourself," Michael said. "What did you have to do?"

"Quite a bit, actually. Flooring, walls, and some of the roof. Would you like a coffee? I just made some."

"Yes. Thank you."

She stepped through the doorway into the kitchen and came back and set a full cup in front of him. He took it black.

"What's this?" She nodded at two little pill bottles on the table.

"It's something for the odd bad night, to help you calm down. And stronger codeine for the migraines. Give them a try." He leaned back and looked around with interest. "And this is where Jack's father killed himself?"

"Not in here. Among the trees down the slope. With a British Army revolver that belonged to Jack's grandfather. The colonel had served in the second Boer War and in the First World War. The gun was locked away and the shells were in a different place, but Jack's father knew where to find them."

"And he took it and shot himself."

She nodded. "That's how much the war had messed him up. He came back an angry and hollow man. He would beat Jack, and then at nights Jack could hear him weeping through the bedroom door and his mother whispering to him. War, Michael. Not the heroic blather that's always followed by the never-again stuff, but the reality of it. Combine that with what I saw in Paris after the war, and you'll see why I feel the way I do."

"Yes, I know."

He waited a moment, then said, "Can we talk about your X-ray for a minute? In the States and in Britain they are working on a new kind of deep imaging system, but it's not quite ready yet. X-rays are not good with soft tissue. Still, at low power settings we can see blood vessels and we can see, or guess at, the denser rims of soft tissue. Like in the brain. We've done yours twice now and the results were always negative. So we just don't know, but X-rays are radiation and I wouldn't want to do another one with you. Chances are your condition will correct itself over time. Until then we should be able to keep it in check with medication, and you can do a lot with what we've been talking about. Stress, blood pressure, moods, exertion, what sorts of thoughts not to allow to come up. I am not saying it's all mind over matter, but it's worth trying."

"Are you sure it's not what my mother had?"

"Reasonably so. I don't see any suspicious widening of blood vessels. Are they being helpful at the pain clinic?"

"Yes. Zach is teaching me about Japanese techniques. And he wants me to concentrate on the good side of my brain and talk to the pain like I would to an animal. Kindly, firmly."

"Well, why not? If it works. Zach is different, but he's good." He nodded at the pills on the coffee table. "When it gets too bad, take one. Just one. They can be hard on your stomach and kidneys."

"All right. Thanks."

"Tell me more about you and Jack. About the phone call."

"This time there was an edge to his voice. That's new. And I rarely see lights on at the house any more. He used to come home between assignments, but now I think he often flies straight from one to the other. Sometimes I find a note, telling me where he is."

Michael sat back in the chair. He looked at her face, at the black silk mourning band on her sleeve.

"Have you deliberately cut yourself off from him?"

"Not exactly cut off, but withdrawn. I tried to explain it to him."

"Margaret, you do know that I talk to him once in a while. Is that still all right?"

"Yes, it's all right. It's even helpful to know. You're kind of like a bridge."

"Good. Jack says you didn't explain much at all, but also that it was not necessary. He understood, or at least he accepted. He asked me, and I told him that withdrawal is the classic overall symptom for women. It's different for men, let's say for Jack, than for you. For him, losing you and his life with you comes on top of losing his son. It's true that mothers feel the loss of a child more keenly than do fathers, but fathers certainly feel it too. Perhaps remember that and don't do anything abrupt. The death of a child is often fatal for a marriage. We've talked about that. And that it's most often the woman who ends it, or causes it to end."

"Do you know why?"

"Because it was her child. It was what she wanted and needed and loved all along. For most women of a certain age, the child comes first. Which is not to say they don't love their man, but the instinct to have and raise a child is very powerful. Unless the couple has something exceptional, the husband is just a part of the overall plan. But Margaret, I think that you and Jack do have something exceptional, so just bloody well hang in there and keep fighting. At least until you have a bit of distance."

For some time they sat in silence. They could hear a squirrel chattering up in a tree somewhere.

"The first year is the hardest, Margaret. After that your chances improve. Statistically."

Michael was a family friend by then. For a while, when she'd thought she needed a second opinion, she'd seen Dr. Robson, but Robson had been useless. Too young, first of all. Too full of recent learning that had yet to settle into knowledge and experience. He'd used the word *hysterics*, and then had quickly added, "In the classic Greek sense, you understand. Etymology. The root word *hystera*, as in womb, for woman, for an excess of emotion and a lack of control."

She'd never gone back to him, although the possible slip into something close to hysterics was a dark companion for a while, a tempting escape from reality. Especially once she'd begun suddenly to glimpse Andrew across the street, his posture, his walk. Or in a subway car from behind, because, since he hadn't come home and hadn't been in that coffin, where was he? And he'd never said a real goodbye. For that last trip they picked him up in a grey military bus at the top of their road in Sweetbarry, and he was happy, laughing, so heartbreakingly thrilled. She and Jack had flown out to spend Christmas with him, and on that last day they'd walked up the snowy road and at the top Andrew hugged them and gave her a peck on the cheek and then he shouldered his kitbag and climbed on the bus and the door closed. She never even saw him waving from a window.

"Dear Margaret," said Michael. "Would it help you to switch to this? Perhaps to suggest some change or progress to yourself?" He reached into his jacket pocket and took out a lapel pin in the form of a small black bowtie and put it on the table.

"You brought this for me?"

"I did. I thought it might help."

She sat holding it in her hands, looking down at it.

"Dear Margaret . . ." he said again. Then he said nothing for some time. Eventually he reached for his doctor bag and set it in his lap. "Jack's a good man, you know. But I don't need to tell you that. How is your sleep?"

"Not good. It's fragmented, and I have dreams."

"Dreams can be helpful."

"I dream of my childhood. Of my school years in France. Of Jack and me early on. And of Andrew. I think I'm searching my past to see if there's anything that might help me now."

"And is there?"

"Perhaps."

She could tell he was waiting for her to say more, but she didn't. Eventually he stood up.

When he left, he paused in the open door and looked out over the garden and the trees and the back of the main house in the late light. "Beautiful," he said.

"It is. When the colonel's family first came here, they were so British they kept peacocks. Until the neighbours complained about the noise, and then they switched to pheasants."

"Pheasants! They couldn't shoot them, surely. Could they?"

"No. They hired someone to make it nice for the pheasants, and they imported the right food so the birds would stay. Heated stalls for the winter. And they imported English roses and planted these quince bushes. At one time there were many more. Jack's mother made quince jelly. I did too, the first few years."

She watched him leave. The sun on his back and on his greying hair, the hair stirring a bit in the breeze. She stood in the doorway until she couldn't see him any more.

Five

ON MONDAY WHEN SHE CAME home from the office, there were lights on at the main house. She could see Jack in the bright rectangle of the kitchen window, and she knew that, were she to hurry up there now and say his name and open her arms and mean it, he would turn to her and she would have reached straight through to his heart. And yet, when she had climbed the stairs and was in the kitchen and had set down her bags, she could not do it.

He stood watching her reflection in the window, and she stood shielding her eyes against the bright ceiling light, the gleaming tiles and white appliances.

He turned. "All this distance, Maggie. We're forgetting how to be with each other. You must know we can't go on like this. If you need help, would you please just go and get it."

"I have help. I have Michael, and I have Zach at the pain clinic. They are both very good."

"And?"

"And nothing. These things take time."

In the bright light her vision began to shimmer, and she closed her eyes and stood rigid for a while. Not now, she said to her eyebrow. Not bloody now. She groped in her purse and took out her sunglasses and put them on. In her own kitchen, in this brutal glare.

"Can we go in the living room, Jack? It's too bright in here."

"Sure. How are you doing with the headaches?"

"I am getting help with them too. How are *you* doing? *What* are you doing?"

"You know what I do, Margaret. I go down mine shafts and I design geophysics and study core samples. I miss Andrew, but keeping busy with what I'm good at helps me. You know all about that particular trick."

In the living room they sat far apart on the same couch. There was a newspaper on the floor that Jack must have picked up. In the photo under the headline about the Camp David peace talks, Jimmy Carter stood side by side with Anwar Sadat and Menachem Begin.

Jack looked at her. "How are you really, Margaret?"

"Honestly? Sometimes not so good. There are long

moments when the entire world slides away from me and all I can do is watch it recede. The other day I had this feeling even at the office, where I'm usually safe. I dream that it's my fault. Not paying enough attention to him. Our boy, killed in some conflict halfway round the world that he had no need to be in. And then I think it's because we didn't help him plant his roots deep enough in common sense. You and I, Jack, we failed at that."

He shifted on the couch and without looking at her he said, "You need to stop that, Margaret. Always the same litany, we did this and we did that. We neglected whatever. When in fact his mind was made up and he'd stopped listening to us years ago."

Which was true, and she knew it.

All those young pilots in training at the Air Force base in the valley coming out to the coast, summer after summer. Young men not much older than he, and some of them already observers or even co-pilots. Andrew had always admired them from a distance, and when he was at university working toward his engineering degree, he made a few friends among them. Sometimes they'd visit, and they'd sit in her kitchen and she'd make lunches for them, proper young men with a calm confidence about them. Once in a while one or two of them would bunk in the boathouse for a summer weekend, and then some of them would invite

Andrew to the base so he could watch the enormous Hercules C-130 machines taking off and landing. The RCAF was being re-organized; new units were being formed that were looking for pilots, and during his last year at university some of those units were prepared to enlist and train fit young men who hadn't gone to the military college but had studied engineering.

One day they let him sit as an observer in a cockpit when a plane did a turn around the valley, and she'd never forget the expression of awe and wonder on his face when he described it to her and Jack.

All those young men in uniform, skilled and disciplined. Boys about to become pilots. That was what he wanted, and he would have succeeded. They offered to sign him up as a trainee even while he was still writing the last paper for his degree, and from that moment on there was nothing she could do any more. Nothing.

Not for war but for peace, he'd say to her more than once in the weeks and months that followed, to soften her. Peacekeeping missions, Mom, all of them. Bringing medicines and clothing and food to people who need help. What could be wrong with that? And he'd watch her face, not the way he'd done as a little boy, but more and more from an inner certainty and decidedness that she recognized only too well because it was in her also and always had been.

—

Jack stood up and opened the window and sat down again. A breeze stirred the leaves on the maple tree and cool air blew in.

From his place far away on the couch he said, "Wouldn't it help you to look at it from his point of view for a change? Flying those amazing machines halfway around the world to exotic places, even into danger—yes, that's part of it, and you rely on your training and your discipline. What a thrill it must have been for him, Margaret. Why not let him have that? And then from euphoria to nothingness in a few seconds. Sometimes I think we should all be so lucky."

She reached for a tissue in the box on the end table and dabbed her eyes. After a while she said, "I know you think that. You've said it before, and it wasn't any help then and it isn't now." She balled the tissue and held it in her fist. "But l want you to know that I'm hanging in with all my broken fingernails. Until I can see more clearly. I'm determined to. I just have to find a way."

"I know, Margaret."

"And it may take a while."

For some time they sat in silence, then she stood up.

"I brought something from the Thai place. Let's eat."

She carried in plates and cutlery and set the cardboard containers on the bare table.

"What is it?"

"Chicken with rice and chestnuts and mushrooms."

They passed the cardboard containers. The serving spoon. Twice their fingers touched. It was the closest they'd been in a long time, but the touch felt wrong to her. Too soon. Somehow inappropriate.

The watch on her wrist was still the good Swiss automatic he'd bought her years ago on an anniversary trip to New York. She looked from her hands to his, and the wedding band was still where she'd slipped it on his finger all those years ago.

She'd met him in her second year at Osgoode Hall Law School, at the cow gate at the Queen Street entrance. He was so engrossed in it, she had to stop and watch him operate it, crouching down to observe the assembly, the way the thing worked. A simple machine of enamelled cast iron, it seemed to her. She watched for a while because there was something she liked very much about him, perhaps the quality of his attention. She stepped closer. "Is there something wrong with it?"

He looked up. "What? No, no. Nothing's wrong. It's just

this amazing piece of history. I mean, look at it. And could there really have been cows grazing here at one time? Cows, here?"

That had been the beginning. In order to find out everything she could about him, to see him clearly in a cool light, she held back for months and would not allow intimacies beyond perhaps a touch of fingers or a kiss on the cheek, but already she was crazy about him. She enjoyed talking with him because Jack talked straight from the heart and looked you in the eye, and unlike with many of her fellow students, everything he said seemed pure and there was nothing hidden in his words ever.

She brought him home and Father liked him as well, approved of him and of his plans for the future. A mining geologist he was going to be, not a soldier like his father and grandfather. As they sat at the dinner table in the house on Colin Avenue, she watched his hands shaping and describing strata and outcroppings to Father, and all the while her brain had stopped and she was imagining those very hands undressing her in some fine cool bedroom, and her undressing him. At that moment much of the fear about intimacy after Lakewood and Thérèse's warnings in Paris about boys and men went out the window. Because here was the real thing, Jack Bradley and his power of attention, and Jack's well-shaped hands and how would their touch feel on her skin?

She told Aileen about her mining geologist with the brown eyes and the good hands on the telephone from Toronto. So excited, both of them. Aileen was engaged to Don Patterson by then, who had steady work on fishing boats off the South Shore. They were doing it, said Aileen. Of course they were. It was so sweet that a few times she'd practically fainted. For birth control she was using the rhythm method, the Knaus-Ogino. Aileen said she'd done her research and under the right circumstances it was the best and she was very, very careful counting days and keeping an extra two days as buffers toward the middle. But in any case, they would be getting married as soon as they had saved enough money. By then Aileen had already passed her exams and she was a fully qualified nurse at Clearwater Hospital.

They agreed that the Thai food was good. An interesting flavour. All that coconut milk, probably. Jack talked about Argentina, and he was describing the silver mine going down and down four levels when the telephone rang. He stood up and went to answer it and then she heard him in the hallway. "All right," he was saying. "I understand. I'll check my schedule."

He came back and sat down. "That was the Vancouver office about the forward core samples on the new silver mine. They want me to come out there for the evaluation." He paused. "Unless you'd like me to stay here a day or two longer. I could probably arrange that."

When she said nothing, he put his hands flat on the table and prepared to get up. But then he sat back again.

"Margaret," he said. "We need to move on from where we are, where we are stuck. Can't we do it together? As a team?"

He sat looking at her, waiting. After a while he shook his head. "You see. There it is again. Your silence. Your unwillingness to meet me halfway. And we used to be so close. We could talk about anything and work out every last problem. We're mature and we can think. So let's please help each other."

Surely there was something she could be saying now. Should be wanting to say, if only she could see it clearly. Perhaps that she felt the same way but that she was lost and couldn't find her way back. That she sometimes wished she were dead, and that what she felt was much deeper and older, and if Michael was right it was even primal and mostly female, with no way across the divide that she could see. And suddenly she could not breathe again . . .

Abruptly she pushed back her chair and stood up and touched her eyebrow.

"So would you like me to postpone British Columbia?" he said. "Stay a bit longer?"

"Maybe not just yet, Jack. But thank you."

He sat watching her, and he never said another word while she fumbled up her plate and cutlery and took them to the kitchen and then picked up her briefcase and purse and hurried away, down the back stairs to be alone again.

She walked with the fingers of her left hand pressed to her eyebrow and talked to it. No, she told it. Not now. Please. But it was not listening and the pain expanded and became the red cloud, and then on the path near the cottage she fell but managed to get up and make it through the door. She dropped the briefcase and with her hand pressed to her mouth ran to the bathroom and in the dark fell to her knees by the toilet and vomited into the bowl. For a while she hung over the rim, then she let go and lay face down on the tiles with her feet out the door and her nails digging into the grouting for a finger hold or keep falling. She pressed the offending eyebrow to the hard ceramic chill and concentrated on the calm side of her brain.

After a while she rolled over and put the palms of her hands over her eyes to make it all even darker. Lying flat on her back in her black suit with her legs outstretched, like some thing fallen from a great height.

After a while she stirred and poked the emergency pill out of her jacket pocket. She bit on it and moved the crumbs under her tongue and let her arm fall to her side.

When the pain began to lessen she rolled over and stood up slowly. She turned on the small mirror light and took off her jacket and slapped away the floor dirt. She slapped angrily at the skirt too and then washed her hands and rinsed her face and mouth, refusing to look up into the mirror.

She could have talked more to him just now. Slowed herself down and said something kind when he offered to delay his trip for her. An explanation, but of what, using which words? And not with this pain coming.

So much change. If she were to step out the door now and look toward the elderberries, she'd see the spot where Jack and she made love for the first time. Finally letting go had been such an enormous event, so very daring and liberating at the same time.

Just down the slope a bit, in the grass.

Late summer, a Saturday night. They'd had dinner with his mother, who did not talk much any more—not since *the event*, as his father's suicide had been called. After dessert they sat a while longer, then they excused themselves. He kissed his mother on the cheek and Margaret said, Thank you for dinner, Mrs. Bradley, and good night, and then they left her sitting at the table. Like a shell. Abandoned. Margaret paused at the door and, feeling guilty, turned back to say something more, but the woman was not looking at her and there was really nothing more to say. In the kitchen the maid, Anna Maria, was washing dishes and Margaret called out good night to her, and then like giddy children they hurried down the back stairs and along the path and past the cottage all in darkness, deeper into the garden.

Watching Jack across the dinner table talking to his mother, watching his face and seeing the care in it, she'd fallen in love with him all over again and she'd made the decision, or it had made itself. At one point Jack looked at her, and he must have seen it in her eyes or in her smile. And he stopped talking and got all red in the face and lost his train of thought.

And how perfect it was.

For a while she was still conflicted even though she knew it was a safe day, but how sweet even that, giving herself permission to let go. In the dark amid the scent of the grass, a sliver of moon and a million stars, starlight like milk on their skin. And his hands on her, finally. And hers on him, completely overwhelmed by all this.

How long ago? Not so very long. Not so long.

THE CHILDREN

Six

ON MONDAY EVENING Aileen saw the lights of the police boat heading out, red and blue lights flashing, and briefly she could also hear the sound of the engines. She watched from her window as the lights moved away and eventually she lost them on the horizon. The police boat, going where?

Next morning, when she was up in the roadside blueberry patch, a car came her way trailing dust. It slowed at the turnoff, drove past it, then stopped.

She shielded her eyes with her hand to see against the low sun. The car backed up and turned into their gravel road. A black car with wide tires and something mounted on the dash. The sun gleamed on its side and dust danced around it. Small stones leapt away from the rolling tires. She saw all this with an ominous clarity, the black car and the way it came rolling into her world.

There was just one man in it, a man in a suit jacket and a blue shirt and tie, and he turned her way going past and gave a quick nod and drove on. On the rock shelf in front of her house he stopped and climbed out and looked around.

Franklin was there, working on her Vauxhall, and he saw the man and put down the tools and spoke to him. There was a short exchange and then Franklin looked her way and waved an arm for her to come down.

She took up the blueberry pail and climbed slowly down from the rise onto the road, holding on to plants and roots. She was annoyed at the interruption. Her hands were blue and sticky, and she was dressed not for company but for picking, in a windbreaker and a balding pair of corduroys and her old boots.

Franklin had gone back to working on the car, and the visitor stood waiting for her by the picnic bench. Under one arm he held a yellow file folder, and he reached into his jacket pocket and took out a card. He held it out to her.

"Inspector Jack Sorensen, Mrs. McInnis. I was hoping to find your son Danny here."

She took the card and looked at it.

"And what's this all about?"

"We want to talk to him."

"What about?"

"Ma'am, is he here?"

"No. Danny doesn't really live here any more. He just visits."

"He owns a boat, right? And he looks after summer properties in the off-season?"

"Yes, he does do that."

She put the card on the picnic table and stepped to the outside tap and turned it on. She rinsed her hands and then took her time with the towel, hoping it would calm her.

Over her shoulder she said, "Danny is a grown man and I'm not checking up on him any more."

"But surely you know where we can find him."

"Well, no. It depends on which loop he's doing. North or south, and in his truck or in the boat." She hung up the towel and turned to him. "The boy is busy and he often stays over at places."

"When was the last time you talked with him?"

"That would be a few days, maybe a week now. Maybe more. A good while, anyway."

"You don't know how long ago, Mrs. McInnis?"

"No. Not exactly."

He stood looking at her, taking his time, and she disliked him for his calm, for the trouble he was bringing.

"All right," he said finally. "If he calls or shows up, please tell him to call the number on the card. Or call Sergeant Sullivan at the station. They'll find me. It's important."

"You still haven't told me what it's about."

"Ma'am. Your son is wanted for questioning by the police. It's as simple as that."

He nodded at her and then climbed into his car, closed the door, and started the engine. He didn't bother to look at her again, just made a three-point turn with pebbles grinding on the rock and drove off.

She walked over to Franklin where he stood by the open hood of the Vauxhall, watching her, holding a rag and a spanner.

"What was that all about?"

"A policeman. Wants to talk to Danny."

"Did he say why?"

"No. Wouldn't give an inch." She felt upset, and before Franklin's questions could make it any worse she changed the topic and nodded at the car. "What's it this time?"

"Same old thing. The electrics. I think you should replace the cables and the distributor cap. The cables get brittle and the cap gets cracks, and when it's damp the sparks go everywhere. I never understood why you had to buy one of these foreign things anyway."

"Because it was cheap and I needed a car. What's that going to cost, Franklin?"

"Not much. Sixty or seventy at the dealership."

"That's still a lot," she said. "Nine years ago the whole car cost just a thousand new. Can you fix it for now?"

"I did already."

He leaned into the cabin and started the motor. It ran a bit ragged at first, then it smoothed out. In the darkness of the engine compartment she could see electricity, blue like St. Elmo's fire, crawling around the distributor cap and along the wires.

Franklin grinned at her. He picked up his tools and wrapped them in the rag and left.

Less than two hours later he was back.

He and another man stood knocking at her door and when she opened, Franklin said, "You know Galway. I bumped into him at the marina just now. He has quite a story, and I said he should tell it to you because I think Crieff Island is one of the places Danny is looking after. Maybe that's why the inspector was here."

They sat in the kitchen and she took beers for the men out of the fridge and uncapped them. Then she and Franklin sat listening to Galway's story and no one interrupted him even once. As she listened she felt cold suddenly, and got colder and colder as his story went on.

Last evening, Galway said to them, he'd been heading home from Medway when his engine developed problems. He changed course to Crieff Island, where he made fast at the floating dock.

He saw some unusual footprints, like blood, he thought, but could it be? So much of it, and he followed them up the ladder to the cribbed dock and then up there he could see it clearly all over the planks, the reflections and the darkness of it. Yes, it was blood. A lot of it. It hadn't rained in days and some of it was dried and soaked into the wood grain, some of it congealed and cracked where it lay thickest.

He walked to the edge of the dock and looked down, and that was when he saw something in maybe four feet of water, snagged in the rocks and beams of the cribbing. He got a hand light from his boat and shone it down. And then he went to his wheelhouse, picked up the phone and made the call.

The police took his name and location and the name of his boat. They ordered him to remain at the scene, and he sat and waited as the sky went from orange to black.

When they came he saw them from far off, the flashing lights, and not long thereafter there was the sound of the big outboards. They made fast on the other side of the floater and told him to remain on his boat. There were three of them. One of them was Sullivan, a local boy but a sergeant now, and he was in charge.

They climbed the fixed dock and looked around and talked about it. They had good hand lamps and they beamed them down into the water, and then they cordoned it all off with police tape and Sully came stepping across the float to talk to him.

"Come aboard, Galway?" he asked, and Galway stood up and said, "Sure, yes, of course."

He gave the boy the transom bench, and he sat down on a lobster crate. Then Sully began asking questions and writing down the answers. He asked about times and conditions, what Galway had seen and his reasons for tying up at the dock. Galway said he was running an old two-stroke engine and the spark plugs kept fouling, and he'd tied up for some quick maintenance.

"Would you happen to know them?" said Sully. "Those two."

"It's hard to tell from up here. But I don't think so. They look like just kids. A boy and a girl, are they?"

"Could be. This is a summer property, right?"

"Yes. I hear it's people from New York that own it. I don't know their names."

"We can find that out. Who is looking after it in the off-season?"

"Not me," said Galway.

"Okay. But do you know who is?"

"No. I don't."

"Want to take a guess?"

"No. But right now there's only a few guys doing the islands. Guys with boats big enough for out here."

"But you wouldn't want to take a guess?"

"And get them in trouble? No, I wouldn't," Galway said.

When the men had left, Aileen went outside and sat for a while on her rock. She had put on a wool cardigan and she sat hugging her knees, looking out to sea. Gull Rock deep red out there in the last sun. The tidal pools like molten silver and the cold sea foaming across rocks that moved and rumbled and spoke in the dark. You had to be quiet inside to hear that.

The very bones of this patient earth laid bare by glaciers long ago, her father used to say. He'd liked reading *National Geographic*. Vast slabs of stone, just look at them, Aillie, he'd say. Bald and smoothed and ancient. Like whales petrified in the very act of breaching. Colossal foundling rocks on these barren shores. Look at them. Rock slabs balancing on other rocks for a thousand years and impossible to fathom how.

She stood up and wiped at the seat of her cords and walked away toward the house. The wind was turning. She could feel it. Backing to nor'east. Something was coming this way.

In her house she kept the cardigan on but kicked off her boots and walked around in sock feet. She heated some of yesterday's stew and then she sat by the window, eating with the light out. Waiting for the fox.

And eventually she heard it. She set down the plate and looked out the window, but there was no moon and she couldn't see anything. But she could hear the fox close by, loud and clear—five, six long yelping barks that most nights still gave her goosebumps and made her smile. But tonight her heart wasn't in it.

Later a wind did come up. She woke and listened to it, and after a while she could tell that it had backed right through the nor'east corner and kept going and it would not be so bad. She could hear the house coming alive and creaking and shouldering the wind, and she felt safe in it.

Her mother's house, and her grandmother's before that. Dorothy Dundonnell from the Island of Mull. Called Dotty. A day labourer's daughter in wooden shoes, come here on a settler boat with a good young husband and a few bundles and a baby in a basket. Her husband worked as a fisherman and she worked in the cannery with the baby on her back, and when they had saved enough money they bought this wooden house and the two-hundred-foot shoreline of rock as their very own, like a dream come true.

The baby would grow up to be Aileen's mother, who had no memory of Mull of course, but she would always know her cradle song, and in time when Aileen was a baby in that same little room under the eaves, the room that was now Danny's, her mother would sit by her crib and sing it softly to her: Speed, bonny boat, like a bird on the wing / Onward, the sailors cry / Carry the lass who's born to be queen over the sea to Skye . . .

For a while Aileen lay listening to those words and to the ones she'd changed them back to with Danny, the lad who's born to be king, and she lay listening to the wind and the waves and to her good house. She tried not to think of Galway's story, and eventually she fell asleep.

—

On Wednesday morning in Toronto, Margaret was at her desk when Aileen's call was put through. She listened and wrote down the names of the fisherman and the detective.

"You really don't know where Danny is?"

"No. He comes and goes. He's busy. Especially this time of year. I think he's looking after more than thirty properties now. People give him keys and he often stays over. Bunks on couches in his sleeping bag. The owners even encourage that because it makes the places look lived-in."

"And Crieff Island is a property that you know he's looking after?"

"Yes, it is."

Already she knew what Aileen was going to ask, and she knew without question that she'd do it.

When she'd hung up she walked down the hall to Hugh's office and knocked and entered.

Hugh, grandfatherly and very rich, sat at his rosewood desk, in one of his suits where even the vests had lapels. He looked up.

"Margaret. Is everything all right?"

"Yes. But I need to take a few days off, Hugh. A good friend of mine on the East Coast needs my help with something."

"Really? But we're very busy right now. You are. The upcoming Hong Kong deal. The Toronto Hydro case, the airport land acquisition. And any day now there'll be that conference call with Chicago. You've got to wrap that up."

"I know, Hugh. I can do all that on the phone from the coast."

"Can you?"

"Yes. I'll bring the files, and if there's the least indication that I should be here in person, I'll be on the next plane. This is important, Hugh. I'd like to catch the one-thirty flight."

"So soon. Really? Hmm. Just a few days, though, right? Because I need you here, Margaret."

"Just a few days, Hugh. Two or three. I promise, absolutely."

She left a note on Jack's typewriter telling him where she was going, and two hours later she sat by a window half-way down the plane as it taxied toward the runway. Rain on the tarmac. Pulsing reflections everywhere.

The small bottle with the new, stronger codeine pills was in her purse, and one of the pills was ready in her jacket pocket. She put on sunglasses and fussed down the window blind and took the glasses off again. She hated flying. The insanity of a rattling aluminum tube stuffed with all these people strapped into their seats miles up in thin air.

Under her the wheels were racing over the cracks in the tarmac now, taking her away faster and faster. Then liftoff.

Seven

THE CAPTAIN'S VOICE came on in English and in French and she thought of her time in Paris, after Lakewood. The day she left Halifax in a new dress and coat and stiff new shoes, she boarded that ocean liner as one person, and nearly five years later she came back as quite another.

At École Olivier, the headmistress's office was in one of the larger cells of what had once been a Benedictine nunnery, with two leaded windows of untrue glass like bottle bottoms. Thérèse was slim and well dressed in a long skirt and a white blouse with a jacket over it. Her hair was black, held up with combs in a French twist.

Near the end of their first talk, Thérèse said, "In private, such as now, you can call me Thérèse. And I will call you Margaret. At all other times I'll call you Mademoiselle like all the other girls, and you should call me Madame. Yes?"

Margaret nodded.

"This school was founded for young women just like you," said Thérèse. "Women, girls from all over who had difficulties or who made a mistake, or to whom a mistake was made, as I prefer to put it. And now they need help. I was one of them too once, Margaret. I was. For the first few years I tried to keep it a secret, but after a while not any more. Secrets burden us. Your grandmother and I don't quite agree on that, but she's of another generation and it's also true that small communities are different."

Thérèse sat back in her chair and smiled at Margaret.

"I know your story, and there is absolutely nothing shameful about it. Some girls feel that there is, but there is not. The only disgrace is that nature feels free to impose it on someone so young and unready—"

There was a knock on the door and Thérèse looked up and said, "Yes?"

The door opened and a young woman came in.

"Ah. Angelique. This is Margaret from Canada. Margaret, we have rules here, of course, and Angelique here will explain them to you and she'll show you around. Please pay attention to the rules. I would not be able to make exceptions. We'll talk more in a day or two."

—

Because she had to make up the time she had missed while at Lakewood, the workload was heavy, but if the girls needed help, and she did, there was access to tutors in the evenings. Thérèse taught philosophy and the classics, and one evening a week she also held a session she called Women's Stories. For those occasions they sat on chairs and cushions in the lounge, and Thérèse sat among them, not as a teacher but as a storyteller and moderator, as a friend almost. They read women's stories, fictional and real, from Madame Bovary to Madame Curie, then discussed them and made up alternate decisions for the characters, leading to alternate developments. Sometimes the girls made up their own stories, often surprisingly dark and fateful ones, which were then read to the class and discussed and resolved in similar ways. During those sessions Thérèse often talked to them freely about women's choices and careers, and about sex and feelings and biology. Often also about what she called the inner self.

"The reason I want to talk to you about these things," she'd said early on, "is that no one else will. People are shy, or they think it's inappropriate or too personal. But that is nonsense. What you need at this stage perhaps more than at any other is frankness and information and the examples of other women's lives and choices to learn from. And all along, remember that none of what we are talking about may be the absolute or the only truth. Truth, not fact. And so in the end you must decide for yourself what you think is right and what is not. For guidance in all that, we listen to what?"

She paused and looked around, and then she put her hand first to her forehead and then to her heart.

"It's as simple as that," she said. "We'll be talking a lot more about it."

But as kind and refreshing as she could be as a teacher, as a headmistress Thérèse was very strict. Once, when two girls from America broke curfew, Thérèse called an assembly and before the entire student body said, "You were told this on your first day here, but I'll tell you again. Break curfew once and you get a warning. Break it a second time and your parents will be notified. Break it a third time and you'll be sent home. No excuses, no discussion.

"Why? Because, if you stood where I am now, in front of so many young women in full bloom—open flowers, you remind me of, waiting for bees to buzz by and pollinate you. But young men cruising the cafés—we know all about them, and they're more like wolves looking for little lambs than bees looking for nectar. And many of you know already from personal experience what can happen then. I see some of you giggling, but this is no giggling matter. Back home your parents are trusting us with precisely that, to get you through these important years in one piece, whole in body and soul, while also helping you to catch up with your education and to gain a bit of self-knowledge. Never be a little lamb. Never. Little lambs get eaten."

In her time at École Olivier, Margaret made many friends, and two of them—Franziska from Vienna and Anne from Geneva—went on to the Sorbonne with her. Two Sundays a month she was invited to lunch at Thérèse's, and along the way on those occasions she met three of what Thérèse called her boyfriends. One was an airline pilot, the next a lawyer, and the third a civil servant and poet. They appeared and then disappeared one after another, and in Margaret's last year it was another man who was often there for lunch, a man named Philippe, a teacher at another school. He was relaxed and funny, and he was a good cook.

Thérèse would have been in her late thirties then, quite beautiful and stylish. One day Margaret asked if she ever intended to get married, and Thérèse said perhaps, and perhaps not. Looking around among her female friends, she said, it was obvious that few people ever found the perfect mate. Or even a tolerable one. Perhaps it was that loneliness and nature's urgings blinded them and too often led them to think they had found the right him or her, until they discovered that they had not. But by then there were children and endless tedious chores and expenses, and life was set on narrow and often unhappy rails indeed.

"Are you still shocked to hear me talking like that, Margaret? I know you were when you first came here, but you've been among us long enough to know how we think and how we like playing with ideas. And when we see shadows from the corner of our eye we like to invite them in and examine them."

Thérèse said that in terms of marriage and children she was not resigned; she was merely taking a rest, like pausing in some kind of never-ending dance. A step back for an overview. Philippe was divorced and very bright and in no hurry whatsoever, and that suited her fine. Her other men had often become angry with her, resentful of her independence. One of them, when she ended their relationship, had actually struck her. The pilot, of all people, she said. She supposed he resented that she was not an airplane responding to his controls. Another suitor had accused her of thinking like a knife.

It was complicated, she said, but fortunately it was also not terribly important. Important was only what one made of it, how one allowed it to affect one.

Eight

WHEN THE PLANE SLOWED and began to bank, she put on her sunglasses and pushed up the window blind. Halifax and the Atlantic Ocean in the distance. Vast stretches of green, a few roads. For a while she sat with the cold surface of the window against her forehead.

Aileen was waiting for her at the arrivals gate. She was dressed in jeans and a wool cardigan and running shoes. Perhaps a few pounds heavier than in earlier memories, but they suited her, and a bit of grey in her hair but still with those clear eyes that looked straight at you, could look right into you. Smart and funny, still with a laugh that made people turn around.

"I came in your car," she said. "Right now I can't trust mine on the highway, and so Franklin put some gas in yours and we took off the tarp. It's running well."

"Good. It can use the exercise."

"There's a few bits that Franklin says I need for the Vauxhall," Aileen said. "Can we stop at the GM dealership to pick them up? He's written it all down. Is that all right?"

"Of course it is."

She put the carry-on in the back seat and settled behind the wheel. She'd been with her father when he bought this Buick brand new. Almost ten years ago, four years before he died. He'd driven it off the lot, tall and straight and grinning behind the wheel.

"I believe this thing will see me out, Maggie," he'd said. "Eight cylinders and so much power. Want me to show you? I'll step on the gas a bit, so hold on."

At the dealership she pulled up next to the parts entrance and waited for Aileen in the car. After a few minutes Aileen came back out empty-handed. She opened the car door and slipped into the seat.

"They aren't stocking those parts any more. Wouldn't you know. But they'll order them from Toronto and mail them to Franklin, and he'll put them in. I paid up front."

"All right. Let's go. Tell me again exactly what happened."

—

Her house in Sweetbarry was the same vintage as Aileen's. Schooner-built, the old people called them, because their pegged structures with ridge beams like transoms and king posts and struts and hangers right down to the sill plate looked like upside-down ships set to meet the prevailing winds, with the steel eyes for fall trusses in place and in line with the anchors cemented into rock. Ships' carpenters built them when there was no more wooden shipbuilding. Three bedrooms, maple floors, and good-sized kitchens.

Her grandmother's parents bought the house a long time ago. They'd come from Paris but were originally from St. Petersburg. Grandmother's name had been Amélie Alexandra. She was good with languages, and when she was twenty, she worked in Halifax harbour as a translator from French, Russian, and German for the Department of Immigration. She married an Acadian man from the town of La Roche on Nova Scotia's French Shore. Monsieur Jules Joubert was an assistant bank manager. They had one child, a son whom they named Charles, a name that worked in French as well as in English. They always spoke both languages at home. When Monsieur Joubert was promoted to manager of a Toronto branch, they moved there, but they never sold Sweetbarry, and from then on they and their family would return to the coast every summer for long visits.

Locally, Grandmother became known simply and rather fondly as AJ, short for Alexandra Joubert.

Margaret was pouring tea for Aileen and herself when out the window they saw a police car pulling up. Sully got out, and a moment later he knocked on the side door and opened it.

"Hello!" he called. "Mrs. Bradley? It's Sergeant Sullivan."

"In the kitchen, Sully!"

He came through the door with his cap under his arm, holding a file folder with both hands in front of him. Sully was one of a group of local boys whom Margaret had known all their lives. Now he was a grown man filling a uniform, with his blond hair neatly combed, showing a flat ring where the cap had pressed it down.

"Oh good, you're here, Mrs. McInnis," he said to Aileen. "I knocked on your door first. I'm looking for Danny. Would you know where he is?"

"No, I don't," said Aileen. "There was a detective here yesterday with a folder just like that. He was looking for Danny too."

"That was Inspector Sorensen. He left it for us to find Danny. I was assigned to the case."

"What case, Sully? Is this about Crieff Island?"

"I'm not supposed to say. You don't have any idea where he is?"

"Not really. He has his loops that he does in the boat, and properties on the mainland that he does in the truck. I told all this to the inspector."

"Like which properties?"

She mentioned some of the owners' names. They sat at the kitchen table, and at one point while Sullivan was busy writing in his notebook, Aileen reached for the file folder and pulled it toward her. Sullivan saw that and quickly put out his hand to take it back, but somehow the conflicting motions sent the folder to the floor, and typed pages and two large black-and-white photographs slipped far out. They all looked down at them.

Sullivan stood up from the chair and crouched and picked up the folder and collected its contents. He sat down again. He was red in the face now.

"You shouldn't have done that, Mrs. McInnis."

"Are those the Crieff Island children?" said Aileen.

"They aren't children. They're young adults."

"All right, but are they the ones Galway found on Crieff? He was here and told us. They are dead, aren't they?"

Sully was sorting his file, pretending not to hear.

"Sully, lad. Answer me. I'm a nurse and I know a morgue picture when I see one. What's all that got to do with Danny?"

Sully closed the file. He looked up at Margaret and then over at Aileen. He put his hand flat to his tunic front.

"Mrs. McInnis," he said. "You see this uniform? I'm a police sergeant now. I worked hard for it, at the college and in the field. If there are going to be problems just because you've known me a long time, I'll have to report that. And if you won't cooperate because of it, then someone else has to take over this case. I was kind of afraid of that."

Aileen sat back in her chair, looking embarrassed now. For a moment there was silence around the table.

To help out, Margaret said, "Sully, I'm sure Mrs. McInnis will cooperate. Of course she will. I think she's just a bit worried about Danny. We both are."

Sully was still red in the face. He looked from Aileen to Margaret and back at Aileen.

"Then please don't do that kind of thing any more. Interfering like that. This is a very serious case. And while this investigation is going on, and from now on in general, you might want to think of me as Sergeant Sullivan and call me by my rank. Maybe the both of you should do that. We spoke to the owners in New York and so we know it's Danny who's looking after the property, and I also notice that you failed to mention Crieff Island among the names you gave me. If you want to help him, then help us find him. You can start by describing his truck and his boat for me."

———

That evening they sat in the living room in Aileen's house, Margaret on the corduroy sofa and Aileen silent and worried in the green velour chair. The window by Margaret's side looked out onto the ocean, and if she leaned forward she could see her property with the little forest planted by her father, and the white boathouse. When she'd been in law school, her father had bought it cheaply from a place up the coast, and he'd taken it apart and rebuilt it down there, anchored on solid rock well above the tide line. For a while it had served as her study during the summers and holidays; later it became a bunkie for guests and for Andrew and his friends, but it was always called the boathouse.

She looked away from it, out past her own reflection in the glass. The sky was the deepest purple and it was covered in stars all the way to the horizon, where they flared in clusters before they drowned in the phosphorescence of the sea.

Behind her Aileen said, "If I don't hear from the boy, there isn't much I can do, is there? He's got nothing to do with those poor dead kids, I'm sure of it."

Margaret turned around. "Tomorrow we'll drive into Bridgewater and talk to the police. Let's find out exactly what it is they want from Danny. If Sully won't tell us, maybe someone else will."

After a while Aileen said, "Danny's never been the same after Don left, you know. Not really. It did something to him. I know it's a long time ago, but it was kind of like a switch in the rails and the track not going straight any more. I mean, Don was his Daddy. And he was a good man early on, or I wouldn't have had any hopes ever. He never lived in this house except off and on, it's true, but once I had Danny he'd often spend the night here. You'll remember that. It all started to change when the fishing got poor and he went to work in the tire factory. The stench of boiling rubber in that place, he used to say, and I could smell it on him.

"You know all that, but I'm just thinking and I'm not defending him, because it was all right for years until the day he heard about the money people were making out west in construction. In the fresh air. Some of his buddies from town had already gone there. And that was that."

Margaret nodded. Don Patterson hadn't worked out for Aileen, and Knaus-Ogino hadn't either. At least not exactly as planned, because one month Aileen had miscounted. That had been the story for the longest time, anyway. But then there had been an evening like this, the two of them in this parlour with a little blueberry wine, and Aileen had admitted to Margaret that she'd wanted a family and had become a bit impatient and careless, letting fate decide. And fate gave her Danny but not Don.

"Thank God I always had a good job nursing," Aileen said. "And I still put in half days and quite often even full days when they call me, and I have the house and my rock and I'm glad I never put a mortgage on any of it. I gave the boat to Danny to help him make a man of himself. Without his dad. Give the boy a reason to stay here and not move away like all the other young people."

For a while they sat in silence, then Aileen said, "The fox didn't come tonight. Or maybe we just didn't hear her. This is usually her hour. This, or a little earlier. I hope she's all right."

"Why wouldn't she be? Have you seen her lately?"

"Yes. Often. A couple of times a week. She still has her two cubs. Sometimes I see them out playing in the sun. Maybe there were too many cars today, yours and then Sully's. All that coming and going."

Nine

THAT NIGHT, OVER IN her own house, she couldn't sleep. She lay in the big bed in her and Jack's bedroom, and through the half-open window and through the very walls she could hear the ocean and the wind in the trees.

She lay listening, not wanting to think of the pale images of the two young people, but the images would not leave her. Those dark eyes. Their pure faces and the young girl's naked shoulders. And both with their hair so black and combed straight back, showing all of the forehead.

At some point she picked up the flashlight on the bedside table and put on slippers and robe and walked through the house. In Andrew's room she sat at his desk, on the driftwood chair he'd made some time ago. The room was almost exactly as it used to be when he was alive. A year ago he'd practically moved here. CFB Greenwood was not far inland, and often he and one or two colleagues from the base would stay here on short leaves.

She looked around at his bed, the desk and chair, Grandmother's old chifforobe with his clothes in it, and the bucket of lead net weights that he used to work out with. The only thing different was the medal they'd given her, the Silver Cross for Mothers, commonly known as the Mother's Cross.

She shone the flashlight on it, there on the wall where she'd hung it, framed behind glass.

Barely out of university and as an observer still in early training to become a co-pilot and eventually a pilot, he'd been on three flights to Africa already, always on United Nations peacekeeping and relief operations for which Canada had been asked to provide support. There were no incidents, and the newspapers didn't even report those missions. But then came the war in Ethiopia where Somali troops had invaded the Ogaden region and laid claim to it. The conflict grew, and soon it involved Russian and American interests as well.

On that last assignment, he'd been on a transport aircraft that carried a field hospital and medical supplies to help ease the suffering among civilians. The landing zone was supposed to be secure, but when the crew climbed out and lowered the ramp, they came under heavy mortar fire.

At CFB Uplands in Ottawa, his coffin came down the tail ramp of the same kind of airplane he'd been on, a Lockheed C-130. But a week or two later a report on an American channel said that ever since Vietnam, many coffins were coming home secretly empty, but with flags on them and salutes, just to make the parents feel better. A TV reporter had snuck into a hangar and opened two of the draped coffins, and the camera had shown them to be empty.

The story was denied by a military spokesman, but in a studio interview on that same channel two veterans said that it could easily be true, and that it probably had to do with the way many soldiers were dying. Not from mere bullets passing through them, but from deadly accurate mortar and artillery fire. In those massive explosions, some soldiers simply disappeared.

"Literally blown away, ma'am," the one veteran had said to the interviewer. His lower legs were gone, and he sat strapped into a wheelchair with a microphone around his neck. "Shredded and evaporated. The human body being mostly fluid, you see. Which doesn't compress, just becomes vapour. The gas expansion and initial speed of shrapnel from a shell being some twenty or thirty thousand feet per second. Sometimes they can't find not even the boots, never mind the dog tag."

It had been as a result of that report that she escaped for a while into the notion of the empty coffin. Only Michael knew about that. He'd listened to her and opened his hands and composed them again and said nothing. Until a few weeks later she herself came to the end of it.

She clicked off the flashlight and sat in the dark for a while. So many gaping holes in her life. Her mother, dead of an aneurysm when Margaret was only eleven. A doctor had made a drawing of it on a piece of paper to help her understand. Like a red river with a bulge in it from all the heavy flow, an eddy getting wider and wider and one day just bursting the bank and flooding all the land.

Then Grandmother. Then her father. Then Andrew and his empty coffin.

And now her wild, true, besotted love of Jack, and perhaps her marriage. She had so loved being married to that man. What had happened to that feeling? Where did it go?

But enough of this. Enough now.

Grandmother had died in this room. In this very bed. Andrew never knew that. It had been a long time before him. Margaret had been twenty then. Twenty, and back for the summer after her second year at university. After all the youthful philosophizing and playing with ideas about life and death and meaning in the absence of God, suddenly came her first loud wake-up call, her encounter with real dying, followed by real death. All of it. The terrible sounds, the disbelief, the panic, and finally the silence.

She would go down to the water and sit in her favourite place on the rock shelf with her eyes closed and the salt wind hard in her face, and try to understand. Sometimes her father would come down and sit with her for a while, and then he'd get up and leave and get to work again, distract himself in his beloved forest.

After Grandmother had been taken away by the funeral people, the bed had remained unmade for days and the slippers had remained on the floor, side by side, ready to receive the feet that would never come again. In the silence of the room, the orphaned slippers more than any other thing bore a message, and she puzzled over it for days until it came to her that if she applied the thinking she was learning in Paris now, the message could be seen to be not about death but about life. It could be seen as a reminder that life was to be used while one had it, used absolutely, used up like firewood in the flames, as the more interesting new writers and philosophers were saying.

On that one notion they all agreed, that there was no use for life other than to live it; to make it into whatever adventure or imaginary game one chose, and when your time was up, it was over and done with and you could take nothing with you. Nothing. Not even your trusty slippers.

She'd sat listening for the ring of truth in that, all those years ago on her rock. And she sat listening for it again now. In this burdened room, for the echo of it.

She turned the flashlight back on and swept his bucket full of lead, the bed, the fancy brass hook shaped like an eagle that he'd found in an antique store and had polished until it shone and then mounted it on the wall as his special place for his uniform.

She stood up from the unbelievable chair he'd made. Sweetheart, she said to him. Sweetheart.

During her time at the Sorbonne she'd lived in a furnished flat in a war-damaged house. Tank shells had passed through the building from front to back. The great holes had once been boarded up, but the boards had since been pried off and people had climbed in and out and stripped panelling and light fixtures and furnishings from the damaged half.

But the side with her apartment was liveable and the lock on her door worked.

It all lent an element of adventure, and the rent was cheap. All the café crowd lived in similar accommodations, or in unheated hotel rooms. Often on Saturdays in the spring and fall, she and Franziska and Anne went out to stroll the streets and to spend hours window-shopping and at the counters at Bon Marché. In the evenings they often sat with others in the noisy cafés. Their favourite haunts were Le Boeuf d'Or and Les Deux Langoustes. They loved Paris by night and by day, and they loved the new ways of thinking they were learning, ideas that could help you see things differently and in this way could change your life.

They lived a few streets from each other, and they studied French and English literature and history and philosophy. They practised as-ifness and absurdism and phenomenism, keeping notes on their progress. They bought black turtlenecks and they wore lipstick and kohl or no makeup at all, and they bought purple berets and put them on in front of mirrors and set them just so.

They learned a great deal from one specific teaching assistant in philosophy, an unpaid Ph.D. docent, young and intense and brilliant. His name was Jean-Charles Manssourian, French of Armenian extraction. For a while Franziska had a crush on him, but he already had a girlfriend, a tall, thin one with a nice smile, who wore only black and no bra.

What Manssourian taught was thinking imported from the ruins of other European capitals and sifted for truth and reinterpreted. Especially now, after the war, he said, when one had learned to see through life so completely, one needed to make the effort to rise above things, in order to see what one had missed before.

Among the established writers and thinkers, he liked best the few who, in his words, were not fixated on existential nothingness, like staring into a hole that everyone knew was empty, but rather they chose to examine the notion of Now what? Here we are, and how do we go forward?

And even something as simple as finding beauty in nature, said Manssourian, or making the effort to brew a very good cup of coffee or to tie a shoelace exceptionally well was more interesting than the empty hole. Courage and a sense of humour had a lot to do with it, he said.

That kind of searching had been everywhere in Paris in those days. So soon after the war, with buildings in ruin on many a street. The smell of rust and wet rubble in the air. With young men on crutches and in wheel-chairs, and the most unfortunate of them without any limbs at all, being wheeled about in barrows or carried in backpacks with their heads poking out, set down on designated café chairs where the uprights protruded above the top rail so that the straps could be hooked over them and keep the bagman from falling over. Someone, most often his mother or father, would put a glass to his lips and let him sip.

Sometimes a wife. There was one blond woman in American jeans and a pilled black sweater and tennis shoes who did this regularly. She still loved her husband, she said brightly right in front of him. Loved his mind and spirit. And understood him, now more than ever. So much so that not only did she still want his child, who would have arms and legs as strong as his used to be, but if one day he were to ask her to help him die, she would do that for him as well. Of course she would.

Throughout the evening she'd crumble tobacco and roll brown-paper cigarettes and tap them and light them and get them going, and then hold them for him between thumb and forefinger. She'd hold the glass to his lips at just the right angle. If liquid spilled, she'd dab his chin with a handkerchief folded to a dry spot. And when it was time to go she'd put down coins for the drinks and a tip, and she'd say good night and shake hands with everyone around the table. She'd crouch and someone would help her into the straps and she'd stand up and walk away bent over, with her husband on her back.

Everyone a philosopher, a seeker, and new thoughts or old, in her days in Paris the investigation into how to live right, how to make a work of art of the brief absurdity that the war had once again shown human life to be was like a virus, an infectious mood. It in itself gave startling colour and immediacy to every moment of the day.

Ten

IN THE MORNING she and Aileen drove inland to Bridgewater, along narrow roads through a world scraped and tumbled by ice ages and hurricanes, past delicate wooden cottages and stands of tall marsh grass and witch hazel with its white and yellow blossoms and seed pods ready to burst this late time of year. Red-winged blackbirds fluttered. Soldier birds, her father used to call them, because of the red stripes on their wings.

At the police station she gave the desk officer her card and said they wished to speak to Inspector Sorensen. The inspector was not in, said the desk officer. He was not based here and came down from the city only when cases demanded it. Could someone else help them?

"The station chief, then," said Margaret.

The officer walked down the hall and knocked on a door, opened it and leaned in.

A moment later they sat facing the station chief across his desk. He was a man in his forties with short brown hair, and he had his tunic off and his sleeves rolled up. His desk was covered with paperwork.

Margaret explained why they were there, and while he listened he looked from her to Aileen and back at her. When she had finished, he nodded and thought for a moment. He picked up her card and read it once more. He looked up.

"You're an Ontario lawyer. This is Nova Scotia."

"I'm aware of that. Is there a problem?"

"Well. I guess not. Mrs. McInnis here hired you?"

"Yes. Or not exactly *hired*, but she asked me to come along. We are neighbours."

He hesitated, then picked up the receiver and dialled a number and said, "Bring me the Crieff Island file." He listened. "At the morgue? I see. Do we have copies of the photographs? Okay, bring them."

The photos and a handwritten note were brought and they watched him study them. He looked up at Aileen.

"I can tell you that we picked up your son two hours ago, and now we've got him over at the morgue for questioning and to see if he can identify these people."

He held up the photographs for them to see, different

photographs from the ones they'd glimpsed in Margaret's kitchen the day before. In these the boy and the girl lay naked to their waists on narrow steel tables.

"They were found dead in the dock cribbing of a property that we know your son is looking after. The owners of the property are Americans. We called them and wired the pictures. They were here only for July, then they flew back to New York. They don't know these two. Would you, by any chance?"

Margaret looked at Aileen, who shook her head.

"No," said Margaret. "We don't know them."

He put the pictures aside and looked at Aileen. "Just so you know, we haven't charged your son with anything. At the moment we're merely asking him if he can identify the bodies and to tell us about the island property. Maybe he can help us figure out what went on there."

"And then?" said Aileen.

"Then he's free to go."

In the car on the way home she said to Aileen, "You know people at the hospital, don't you?"

"I know most of the nurses. When our hospital closed and I was laid off, some of them transferred there."

"Let's go talk to them."

"About what? If the police have Danny, I don't want to get in the way and maybe cause trouble for him. We should just wait, Margaret. For now. Let him come home and tell us what went on."

"The hospital would have the autopsy report. Do you know the pathologist?"

"Only by name. Let it go, Margaret. We know what we came to find out."

"He didn't tell us how they died. You could ask one of the nurses if I could talk to the pathologist. Just a few minutes. What's wrong with that?"

"I don't want to!" Aileen was getting upset. "Stop it, Margaret. I don't want us asking any more questions of anyone. I want to go home and wait for Danny."

Back in Sweetbarry Aileen walked down the path to Franklin's place. He had pulled up his dinghy into what he called his dry dock, a patch of sand between two logs, and he sat in the stern working on the engine. It was tilted up with the cover off, and he was using a small spanner on a bolt head. He heard her and looked up.

"How was it?"

She stepped into the boat and sat down and shook her head.

"What?" he said.

"They picked up Danny to identify the kids at the morgue. The policeman showed us more pictures, and I'm sure I've never seen them."

"Did they drown?"

"He didn't say."

"Well, were the eyes open?"

"Yes."

"Could they have drowned, like from a boating accident? You've seen what drowned people look like in these waters. Waterlogged and dead-white and the eyes either eaten out by crabs or the pupils wide dilated."

"They weren't eaten out and you couldn't tell if they were wide dilated. They were glossy black-and-white pictures. Dark eyes, and they looked like flat stones. Very dark eyes. Dark hair, too. Maybe black. Combed straight back. Naked. They shouldn't show the girl so far down."

"They could have drowned," said Franklin.

"I don't know. They had marks, here."

She put her hand to her chest, and Franklin looked up at her hand. "What kind of marks? From what?"

"Maybe crab damage, but we didn't ask and the policeman didn't say. They're not from here. I just know it."

"Drowned people can look very different, Aileen. Very different." He bent to the engine again. "What about Danny?

Are they going to let him go? He'll probably come home soon and tell you what went on."

"I hope so. I feel badly because when I asked her, Margaret was so quick to come out for this, but now I don't think I want her getting involved any more. You know how she can be when she makes up her mind about something. Now she wants to talk to the pathologist and see the autopsy report. But I said no."

"Oh? Why is that?"

"Because Danny is a good boy and I don't want her, or me, to get in his way."

"No," he said. "I can see that."

She sat a while longer in the boat, looking down at her hands between her knees. No ring on her finger ever, except for a cheap engagement ring in the long ago. Not that it mattered any more, but who would have thought it in the early days?

"How's Jack?" said Franklin without looking up. "Does she talk about him?"

"Not this time."

"It's all still about Andrew, is it?"

"I'm sure it is."

Thick as thieves, Andrew and Danny had been, when they weren't arguing about something. But most of the time they were playmates and buddies and troublemakers on these rocks and in boats, along with Sully and sometimes that other boy, John Patrick Croft, as well. Just a few years difference between them all. In later years some of the fly-boys out from the base had joined in, with summer girls in the mix of it. Then things changed, with Sully away at the academy to become a policeman, Danny getting busy with his properties, John Patrick working on his skipper licence, and Andrew getting his degree and signing up at the base. Suddenly they were all grown up and it was years later.

She looked up and around at the sky. An eerie light to the east. That bright copper colour, with reefs of dark cloud building in front of it.

"You're rocking the boat," said Franklin. "I'm trying to fix this and it's just little tweaks and it's hard enough to see as is."

"Sorry." She sat still. "There's storm clouds in the weather corner."

"I know. It's not coming just yet but it's thinking about it."

Gett'n ready for a punch, was what her father used to say. And he would look up and around, the way she'd just done, and sniff the air and rub his nose, and he'd know within a few days how much good weather was left before the fall storms came raging into their world.

"I'm going to get out of this boat now, Franklin," she said. "So it'll rock a bit, okay?"

Eleven

WHEN SHE'D COME BACK from the police station there'd been two calls on her answering machine, both from Hugh Templeton about the fact that Chicago wanted a telephone conference at nine in the morning the next day.

"Where the hell were you?" he said when she called him back. "I need you to be available all the time or this isn't going to work. All the time means all the bloody time."

"Okay, okay. I'm sorry, Hugh. Usually I'm right here, except for this morning. I'll call Jenny and make sure she has all the numbers. She can set it up for nine Chicago time tomorrow. That's ten o'clock Toronto time and eleven mine. I'll be ready for it and it's not a problem."

"And we don't want it to become one. This is a big deal, Margaret, and I need you to wrap it up good and tight."

—

Later in the afternoon she walked over to Aileen's to see if Danny had come home. He had, and she found him at the back of the house, chopping firewood while another man who looked familiar to her was stacking the split logs. When Danny saw her, he set the axe on the block and waited for her to come closer. Looking at him she could see Andrew; much the same size and build, perhaps not quite as solid, but with good shoulders and strong arms nevertheless, the same short dark hair and an open face.

The other man said something to Danny and walked away. Moments later a truck engine started.

"Was that by any chance John Patrick Croft?" she said. "I haven't seen him in a long time. Is he still working as a skipper in the harbour?"

"Not right now. Mr. Moynihan fired him for some insurance thing, even though it wasn't really his fault."

"Oh? That's too bad. But tell me what happened at the morgue."

"Well, those kids weren't from around here. I know that for a fact."

"What happened, Danny? Start from the beginning."

"The police stopped me near the Chandler place. I was in the truck, and they flagged me down and ordered me to follow them to the station. Then they took me to the morgue in a cruiser, in the back with the bloody doors locked."

"And then what?"

"Well, those kids didn't drown. They were shot dead, that's why the police were all so serious."

"Shot!"

Danny nodded. "They had them in cold drawers and they pulled them out. Both were shot twice right here." He put his hand to his chest. "He right in the middle, she a bit to the side. Two washed-out little holes each. I've never seen anyone so pale. They'd be around twenty, and they're not from here. I didn't know them and I told them that."

"And what did the police say or do then?"

"Not much. They talked among themselves, Sully and his boss and another cop. All very hush-hush. Then they said that an inspector will be coming down and I should take him over to Crieff and show him around. They'll pay for the gas and my time. Tomorrow early afternoon."

"I think I should come along, Danny."

"Really? Why?"

"To look out for you. This is suddenly all very serious. In fact, it doesn't get any more serious. Have you told your mother?"

He said he had, and she was worried.

"I'm sure she is. I'll go and talk to her. Is she in?"

"I think so."

Up in the house they stood in the little hall, and from the back they could hear Danny chopping wood.

"Only if it's really all right with him," said Aileen. "I mean, are you sure it's a good idea? What if they think you came along because he has something to hide? Maybe the police chief this morning thought that too."

"Aileen, you're all upset. Let's sit down a minute."

They sat down at the kitchen table and Margaret said, "That policeman didn't think Danny has anything to hide, Aileen. It's just that we lawyers make them a little nervous. If you don't want me to go over to the island with them, I won't, but I think it would be to Danny's advantage. I'd make it clear to them that I'm there mostly for moral support, but that as a family friend and a lawyer I'll be looking out legally for him as well. Aileen, the police have a lot of power, and this being a murder case they won't hesitate one second to use it all. Just scare tactics alone, hard questions, you'd be amazed. Me being there will make them a little more careful."

They talked a while longer and in the end Aileen agreed. "If you think so," she said. "Just be real careful they don't get the wrong idea, Margaret. Promise me that."

That night in her robe and boots she walked down to the boathouse, through the little forest with the flashlight in one hand and with the other raised to fend off branches before they could strike her in the face. Inside the boathouse she clicked on the overhead light and looked around. Two iron bunk beds with the thin mattresses rolled up military-style to the head end. The old oaken desk and swivel chair from her time, when she'd studied out here for law exams. Bare stud walls, a few electrical outlets.

At the back there was a small room that her father had used for a workshop, and in it stood a shelf with books and papers on it and a workbench and a wooden box of tools. Work clothes hung on nails. A slicker, a woollen jacket, a canvas coverall. Her father's old Truro Feed baseball cap.

She lifted off some of the clothes for the boat ride tomorrow, then turned out the light and pulled the door shut and walked back up to the house.

—

In the morning she sat at the kitchen table with the papers spread out before her. When the conference call came through, she listened to the client's questions and concerns, then began going over them in detail. Once again she took them step by step through the transaction and all the alternatives and consequences. At one point she heard the Chicago lawyer or perhaps the accountant say something and the client said, "No. We don't need that."

She carried on, and in the end she asked the client if there were any more questions and he said, "No, thank you. Not now. We'll get back to you."

The session lasted fifty-two minutes and she wrote that down in her time sheet.

She called Hugh and reported the main points of the conversation. It had gone well, she said. Then she told him she'd be away from the phone for a short while on an urgent matter, and to leave a message if anything happened. The machine was always on.

Twelve

FOR THE BOAT RIDE to Crieff Island, Inspector Sorensen and Sully wore yellow slickers with POLICE printed on the back. She wore her father's old slicker and cap from the boathouse.

They sat in silence on vinyl truck seats bolted to the deck, the inspector on the seat in front of hers. She'd made it clear why she was there, and the inspector had nodded and turned away. Since then he had not spoken to her, but once in a while she caught a quick appraising glance from him. Eventually he turned to her.

"And why do you think that Danny needs moral support, Mrs. Bradley?"

"Because dealing with the police is always unsettling, and it helps to have someone in one's corner. Always, even when one has nothing to hide. I think you know that, Inspector." She smiled at him.

At times the boat passed through patches of mist thick as rain. Water settled on her eyelashes and beaded on the worn edge of the baseball cap. There was no colour to the world but shades of grey, and the only sounds came from the engine below deck and from water lapping against the hull. On one occasion the boat slowed, then stopped and sounded its horn. Out in the fog another horn responded, and moments later the dark shape of a boat slid across their path and disappeared again. They moved on.

"Did you see that?" said the inspector to her. "How does he know what's out there, where he's going? In this muck. Does he have radar?"

"I don't know. Let's ask him. Danny! The inspector is asking if you have radar on this boat."

Danny laughed at that. "Radar. Nah. It's always a tad foggy in this patch, but we're going slow, and I got my ears and eyes and a sounder and this." He tapped the compass housing. "Anyway, she'll clear up in a few minutes."

At the island they tied up to the floating dock, then ducked under the police tape and climbed the ladder to the cribbed dock. There were large brown stains on the planks. In some places they were congealed, in others they'd soaked into the wood grain.

"Nobody step in that," said Sorensen. "Maybe stand over there, out of the way." He reached into his pocket and took out a pair of plastic gloves.

She watched him move among the stains. Twice he went down on both knees and then moved along like that, judging where to set hands and knees, at times bringing his face close to the planks, tracing something with a finger.

Then he stood up.

"Danny," he said. "Be careful where you step, but come and look at this. This imprint here, it's from a shoe with a smooth sole, probably leather, and a rubber heel plate. A dress shoe, I'd say, fairly small for a man's foot. Do you know anyone who wears shoes like that around here?"

"Is that all blood?"

"Probably. Do you know anyone with shoes like that?"

"Not around here. It would be dangerous in a boat, a shoe like that. No traction in it."

"All right. Stand back again."

Sorensen took a flat tool from his pocket and knelt and scraped up blood. Where it lay like uncured paint he put smears of it into different plastic bags. He stood up and looked around.

"Danny, if anything fell in the water here and floated, which way would it drift?"

Danny pointed with his chin. "That way. Probably. Unless there's a storm. And even then."

Under low power they nosed slowly along the shoreline of the island, often with the engine just in idle. Danny kept having to slip it in and out of gear while Sorensen took his time studying where the water lapped on land.

They saw driftwood, seaweed, crab shells, bits of plastic. Yellow seafoam. But then, around the turn into a small cove, Sorensen pointed.

"There! See that? Go as close as you can and hold the boat in place. How deep is it here?"

"Shallow enough so I'll need to watch the prop."

"Are you sure?"

"Yes, I'm sure."

"Sergeant," the inspector said to Sully. "You see that clump of seaweed and those three reeds sticking up, and the black thing behind it half submerged?"

Sully looked. "That over there. Yes, I do, sir."

"So put on gloves and go get it for me."

And Sully took off the slicker and his uniform and shoes and stripped down to his shorts. He did it without hesitation and without looking at anyone. At the stern ladder he waited for Danny to shut off the engine and then he climbed down and waded ashore, paddling with his gloved hands in ice-cold water up to his hips. Another strong local boy with a good chest and shoulders. All-round strength of muscle and bone and sinew from working with boats and ropes and axes all their lives. Shovel work in the gravel pit during high school summers, the hardest work of all.

Andrew had always admired them, had wanted to be strong like these boys and probably a bit wild and reckless like them too. To be accepted by them and later by his military friends as more than a come-from-away from the city. They'd worked out with that bucket filled with lead net weights that was still in his room. Danny could hold the bucket with one arm straight out for nearly two minutes. Andrew had told her that, quite in awe. They'd been in their late teens then, and she'd been able to hear them up in Andrew's room, counting and laughing, and the rattle of the weights and the thump of the bucket.

When Sully came back he was carrying a black shoe. At the stern ladder he passed it to the inspector, who held it up in gloved hands for Danny and her to see.

It was a man's left dress shoe, a leather loafer with a

pointed toe cap and a narrow bangle of yellow metal across the instep.

"Do you know anyone who wears shoes like that?"

"In the city, yes," she said. "But not around here."

While Sully dried himself off with a towel Danny had given him, Sorensen turned the shoe this way and that to study it. Then he put it in a plastic bag and set it out of the way in a corner on the wheelhouse floor.

The sun was out now, warm and clear. A wall of fog toward the mainland and dark clouds and tendrils of rain far away to the east.

On the way back she asked Sorensen if she could take a closer look at the shoe. He gave her his gloves, and she put them on and took the shoe out of the bag. It had an elevator heel, and it was handmade in Argentina. It would have been expensive.

"A bit of a vain man," she said, "who wanted to appear taller than he was. Size eight and a narrow foot. Less than medium-sized for a man. A fairly common shoe in any big city, I'd say. Perhaps on a Latin or Mediterranean foot. But not on a banker or an Anglo businessman. They like brogues with fancy toe caps."

Now he was looking at her with interest. "Go on."

"And there's blood inside it. Under the insole where it's coming off. See? And more brown all the way inside and under the instep. A shoe full of blood, I'd say."

"Yes," he agreed.

"What did the children have on their feet? There were running-shoe prints on that dock."

"Yes, running shoes. We're going to find out whose blood all that is. The kids', and from that shoe almost certainly someone else's too."

She put the shoe back in the bag and peeled off the gloves and set it all on the wheelhouse floor.

"Danny says they were shot."

"Yes, they were. From up close, with a powerful handgun. The bullets had full metal jackets, so they didn't deform much and punched right through him and into her. We think she was standing close behind him. Maybe he was trying to shield her with his body. We know they died from the same two bullets because the pathologist found one embedded near her spine, and he had a hunch and sent the bullet to the lab and in the grooves and cracks in the copper they found traces of the boy's blood. I can tell you all that because it's in the medical report and as his lawyer you could easily find it out yourself."

Danny was not far away and she imagined he could

hear all this. Later, when the inspector was sitting down, she joined Danny in the wheelhouse. He looked grim.

"Margaret, to tell you the truth—I know I said okay yesterday, but now you being here doesn't feel right to me any more. I guess I don't really want you gett'n involved, like asking him anything or talking on my behalf. I know you told him about moral support, but even that, I've decided I don't want it. Don't need it. I'll tell Mom the same thing. She shouldn't even have called you. I'd rather handle this on my own."

"Really? Are you sure? I'm here now."

"Maybe you shouldn't be, is what I'm saying. Yes, I am sure. I got nothing to hide, and I don't want him to think that maybe I do. That guy doesn't miss a thing. He's like a bloody hawk."

She hesitated. "You're really sure, Danny?"

"I am."

"All right. Let me know if you change your mind."

She turned away from him and sat down and hugged her knees and looked out to sea. Water rushing past. She wiped mist from her face and rubbed her hands against her skirt under her slicker, pulled the cap down even further, and stared out to sea again. Worn threads hung from the peak of the cap, water beading on them.

She looked at her watch. Ten past four. She'd talk to Aileen, and then if she hurried she could probably still make the evening flight back to Toronto.

"Inspector." She tugged at his slicker, and he turned around and rested one arm on the back of the seat.

"Have you found out who these children are?"

"No. And they're not really children. Forensics thinks they're about twenty years old. No, we don't yet know who they are. Or where they're from. We're trying to find the parents."

"The parents. Of course. And if you can't find them?"

He shrugged.

When the boat was docked she asked him for his card. He reached under his slicker, took out a card and passed it to her.

"And you?" He held out his hand. "Your card?"

Thirteen

SHE WAS ON the seven o'clock flight. The dinner choices were chicken or beef. She had the chicken. The window shades were down and the cabin lights dimmed, a movie on the screen. The constant drone of the engines.

Aileen had driven with her to the airport and would take the Buick back to the house.

"I shouldn't have asked you to come out," she'd said in the car. "Put you to all this trouble. I should have waited. The boy just doesn't want a lawyer getting involved. He thinks it makes too much of it all, and in truth I have mixed feelings about it too now. I'm really sorry."

"Don't be, Aileen. I understand and it's all right. Danny seems to be in the clear, and I'm glad about it."

It was foggy in places, as it often was on this coastal road, especially this time of year. Stands of evergreens with birches among them, shimmering pale among the darkness.

Trees. When she was little she'd had a book about trees that her father had loved as much as she had. The tamarack leaning kindly to the hemlock. The balsam fir joining in. All of them nodding their heads to the same breeze.

Where the fog was dense she turned on the low beams and the flashers, then a mile later the view was clear again. Aileen fiddled with the radio but the signals were poor. She switched it off.

At the airport they got out and embraced. She caught a glint in Aileen's eye and reached out and gave her another hug.

Less than three hours later she was back in Toronto, in an airline limo already heading south on Avenue Road. Rain against the windows, water splashing up under the car. Night, and the familiar sights of her hometown. Wide intersections, traffic lights, low flat-roofed commercial buildings lining the street. Crossing Lawrence Avenue now, then Eglinton, heading east and south into the pocket of North Toronto where she grew up. Four-bedroom brick homes, mature maple trees lining streets.

Down Yonge Street now, across St. Clair. One of her

better early jobs had been at a law office right here, working on immigration cases and white-collar crime.

Those had been struggling years, tough learning years, years that sharpened and hardened her. Andrew was in primary school then. At that place, her desk was one of two in the hallway near the washroom, and men still buttoning up as they walked past kept knocking papers off her desk and not even noticing.

One day a young woman came in the door and spoke to the receptionist, and the girl then turned and pointed out Margaret.

The woman came up and looked at her strangely. "Yes," she said. "I remember you."

"You do? From where?"

The woman leaned over the desk and with one of the pencils there wrote something on a piece of paper. She turned it around for Margaret to see.

LAKEWOOD, she'd written. She picked up an eraser and rubbed the word out again.

In the Murray's at the corner, they sat in a booth by a window. The woman was slim, with red curly hair and freckles. In the window light her eyes were sky-blue. They were drinking coffee and eating toasted cheese sandwiches.

It was mid-morning and the restaurant was nearly empty, but they spoke in murmurs anyway.

"You could tell me your first name at least."

"You were already in your eighth month when I arrived, and you were gone long before me. I'm Florence."

"Flo. Yes. I do remember you now. How did you find me?"

The woman shook her head. "Just through someone. They said you were doing human rights cases."

"That's a lofty term. I work fourteen hours a day doing prep work on immigration and white-collar crime files."

"Back then did you have a baby girl or a boy? What colour was its hair? And did it have all its fingers and toes?"

She stared at the woman.

"No idea, right? Because near the end there was the gauze mask and the spray of chloroform. And then it was all over and the baby was gone. Snatched away so fast. Straight to formula."

Margaret wiped her fingers on the napkin and sat back. "What do you want from me?"

"I don't have a lot of money, but I want to hire you to negotiate with them and get the girls holding rights. Twenty-four-hour holding rights, so they can see their babies and hug them. Cry if they want to, but make peace with it. Say hello and goodbye. They can choose not to, but they should have the option."

"Holding rights."

"I made up the word."

"It's not common practice. I imagine to avoid attachment and to make it easier."

"Easier for whom? The clinic? Not for the mother or the baby. The baby knows nothing of anything for weeks, as long as it's swaddled and fed. It's busy learning to breathe, for heaven's sake. No, this would be for the mother. It's a chance I would have loved to have."

Florence looked out the window for a moment, then back at Margaret.

"I can get you two Ph.D. psychologists who'll testify that holding rights would be a good idea for the long-term emotional health of most mothers. To help them stop wondering for years and years what the baby looked like, and was it a boy or a girl and was it healthy. How would it have felt to hold that little bundle."

"Maybe she doesn't really wonder about any of that. Maybe she's made her peace with it."

Florence looked hard at her for a moment, then looked down at the table. She tapped a finger on it. Wiped away some crumbs and looked up.

"Are you married? Did you have other children?"

She nodded yes. "I have a little boy. He's seven."

Florence nodded. "Makes all the difference, later. Trust me, I know. And what I also know is that holding their babies, they would all weep. But a healthy weep, a good long cry of enormous release. You think about it. At least they should have the option. That's all I'm asking."

She reached into her purse and put a slip of paper with her name and number on the table.

"Call me and I'll give you the names of the psychologists. And tell me what it'll cost."

By the time she was back at her desk she was already considering how to go about it.

The next day, searching for leverage, for something to trade with, she did some research into Muskoka zoning and property tax structures, and the following evening after hours she placed the first call to Lakewood. Someone she did not know answered, but when the matron came to the telephone it was clearly still the same woman. That same crisp voice.

"*Holding rights*. What on earth are you talking about? What was your name again?"

"Margaret Joubert. I was at Lakewood in the fall and

winter of 1946 into '47. I'm a lawyer now, and my married name is Margaret Bradley."

She mentioned the name of the law firm. "I can come up on Saturday by car and tell you what I'm proposing."

"I'm not interested in any proposal, and I'm never in on weekends."

"Yes, I remember that. So make an exception. You'll want to hear this. I know you will."

It took five meetings, the first two on her own time, the others on the law firm's time, but as a pro bono case. Her psychologists presented their findings without mentioning names from their own cases, findings that met great resistance because they clashed with Lakewood's long-standing house rules.

In the end it was the forensic accountant who persuaded the matron. Margaret's firm had used him before as an expert in white-collar crime. He never smiled, and somehow that made him all the more effective. He told the matron that he had looked into public records and learned that Lakewood was enjoying non-profit benefits, when a close audit and an evaluation of bookkeeping practices could probably find years in which the business had in fact made a profit.

The business, he repeated.

Because in that case, he said, Lakewood could be viewed as a profit centre that had lost money in some years, rather than a non-profit centre within a corresponding favourable tax bracket.

And so during the fifth meeting a clause was added to the intake form with Yes and No boxes that gave the girls the right to decide in their eighth and ninth months whether they wanted to make use of the new holding right.

She never charged Flo for her time, but she accepted her offer to pay for the experts. In a handwritten note some time later, Florence told her that on average fourteen out of twenty girls ticked the Yes box. The note was signed, *Thank you, thank you, thank you! Sincerely yours, Florence.*

She kept the note in her desk drawer for a week and then she photocopied it and described the situation and sent it to Thérèse in Paris.

She was not surprised when Thérèse wrote back that she could completely understand the girls who ticked the No box. That she'd thought there would be more who said no, with quick angry strokes, and that she could probably guess the stories of those who had.

"Almost certainly not a mere mistake with a fresh-faced

summer boy, dear Margaret," she wrote. "But probably a story more like mine."

On one memorable occasion in her last year at the Sorbonne, she and Thérèse had talked about their stories, as they called them. Thereafter by tacit agreement nothing more was said, mostly because even though the outcomes were the same, their stories themselves were not. They were very different.

Margaret's main memory of Thérèse's story was of one horrific confrontation in her parents' living room: her mother, her father, the father's so-called friend at first in red-faced denial and then in shame, and Thérèse, at seventeen, having told her parents about her condition and how it had come about in half-hearted confusion but in truth against her will. There had been a bruise on her right upper arm that had turned deep purple and would not go away.

"You asked me what I think of those Yes or No boxes," Thérèse wrote near the end of her reply, "and I think that perhaps the idea is wrong because it forces the girls to think about having to choose when the entire thing might be a nightmare for them already. Nature has no interest in our happiness, dear Margaret. So that is what I think. But it's possible that I am still unable to see it clearly."

Fourteen

THAT NIGHT BROUGHT the first of the fall storms to Sweetbarry. Aileen woke from the rapid drop in air pressure, and she got out of bed and stepped to the window to see if Danny's truck was there. It was not. She went back to bed and lay waiting. When the storm made landfall it whistled in her leaking windows and howled in chimney stack and vent pipe. The house shook and creaked, and then the rain and sea spray thundered on the roof and quickly overflowed the eavestroughs.

By morning all was calm again, but a stunned and eerie feeling remained in the air, as of some catastrophe not yet over. From the parlour window she could see Franklin beachcombing in his dinghy, looking for useable stuff. Often after a storm he found all kinds of glass and cork floats and lobster traps that tourists from the cities paid good money for. A painted net float in half-decent condition was worth as much as ten dollars, more if it still had a number painted on it.

The bucket under the leak in her bathroom was half full, and she carried it downstairs and emptied it off her stoop. Then she spent some time picking up the broken shingles that the wind and rain had knocked off her roof.

She was checking if the house had shifted on the foundation blocks and was glad to see that it had not when Franklin came up the path. He was carrying a package.

"From the dealership," he said. "Came this morning. So quick. Let's put it in."

"All right. But have a coffee first."

He shrugged off his coat and kicked off his boots. They had one perked coffee and then another, and some blueberry muffins that she'd made the day before. At one time she handed him a napkin and pointed, and he wiped blueberries off his chin.

"From which patch?" he said.

"Up by the road. I saw the owl and she saw me too. Sat up there and didn't stir a feather. Just looked down at me past her beak, you know how they do that."

Franklin nodded and chewed and swallowed.

"We've got to do the fall wires," she told him. "There'll be more and more storms now and they'll be getting stronger. Don't wait so long again, like you did last year."

"I won't. But one of the turnbuckles has a crack in it. I need to get that welded first."

"Well, you better do that then, Franklin. Before we all get blown off these rocks."

They carried the tool box outside and cut the tape on the package and then laid the distributor cap and the wires and the new spark plugs out on the rock.

Franklin took out the old plugs and showed her the difference. "All shiny and new. They'll last you another seventy thousand."

She chuckled at that.

He cleaned the rotor contacts and clipped on the new cap and connected the wires and pushed the ends down onto the spark plugs.

"You didn't say anything about new spark plugs too," she said. "Or did you? I thought only the cap and the wires."

"No, I think I did mention the spark plugs. And I wrote them down. You paid for them already. Crank her up and let's have a listen."

She swung open the door and slid halfway onto the seat with her right boot on the gas. She inserted the key and turned it.

"Nice," said Franklin. "Listen how smooth. Like a new car, Aillie."

He wiped the fender with his hand and lowered the hood and let it drop gently just the last inch.

"Did Margaret leave?"

"Yes, last night. I drove her to the airport. Feeling like a false friend, asking her to drop everything and come all this way only to have her find out we changed our mind and she's not wanted. She's never been not wanted here. Never."

"It's not like that and you know it. She knows it too. It's much more complicated."

"I suppose it is."

From ten-thirty to two that day she did a pinch shift at the hospital, and when she was back home she took off the nurse's uniform and put it on a hanger in the bedroom closet. It was a sky-blue dress with a white collar and cuffs, a white bib apron, and a white cap. Nursing, that good and noble profession. It had been her life, especially after Don had left, and it was still her life, even if it was only part-time now. It was how she thought of herself. A nurse. You are a nurse.

She shut the closet door and at that moment she heard noises on the rock. Quickly she put on her housedress and stepped to the window. But it wasn't Danny. It was a car she'd never seen before. A city car, clean and new-looking. Two men in trenchcoats were standing next to it and looking around. One of them nodded toward her front door, and a moment later she heard them coming up the stoop. There was a loud knock on the door.

"Coming," she called. "Coming."

She always had to be careful going down those steep wooden stairs, and by the time she got there they were already in her house. They looked at her and only one of them was smiling. He looked pale to her and he stood with his left hand in his coat pocket.

"Oh," said the other. He had reddish hair. "There was no answer and the door was open. We are looking for John Patrick Croft. Is he here?"

"The skipper. No. Why would he be here? Are you from the police again?"

"The police," he said. "Yes."

They stood staring at her. City people. Foreign-looking, but maybe from Montreal or Toronto. Close haircuts and suits and white shirts and narrow ties and shined leather shoes like businesspeople. The one with his hand in his coat pocket was still smiling, only now his smile looked frozen and disconnected from his eyes.

"Dan McInnis, then," said the other. "Is he here? He works with John Patrick."

"Danny isn't here either. He doesn't really live here any more. Not all the time. I'm his mother."

"Are you. Then please give us his address. And John Patrick's too."

"What's this about? The other policeman said Danny was in the clear."

"In the clear about what? And which policeman was that?"

It was beginning to feel all wrong to her then. And she couldn't help looking at their shined, pointy shoes. The three of them stood on the rug in her little foyer and for a while there was not a sound anywhere.

"What policeman?" the man said again.

"I never knew his name. Do you have a card or something?"

"What policeman, and what did he want?"

"I think he was looking for John Patrick too."

"You think," said the one with the red hair. "Why was he looking for John Patrick?"

"Maybe he wasn't. I don't know. You aren't from the police, are you?"

"Aren't we?"

The other one still didn't say anything. He just stood smiling at her.

"We'll have a quick look around," said the redhead. "You stay here."

They shoved her aside and squeezed past in the narrow space, and as they did so, the smiling one bared his teeth, just the upper ones, in a strange thin-lipped curl, and as he pushed past her his trenchcoat and jacket opened and she saw the pistol, large and black in a holster against his shirt.

She made it to a kitchen chair and sat down. She could hear them up in Danny's room, talking in a foreign language. Not French. Perhaps Spanish, she thought. Their shoes loud on the wood floor, scraping and banging noises. Next she heard them in her own room and then in the tiny spare room and the bathroom. They came down and looked around in the parlour and then stood in the kitchen doorway.

"Where do they keep the boat?" said the one with the red hair.

"I don't know."

"Sure you do. You're his mother. Of course you know. Where?"

"No, I don't know. I'm telling you. This is Danny's busy season and so he's probably out on the water with it. I don't think John Patrick even has a boat."

"Don't you? You know what *I* think? I think you're lying to us. Why are you lying?"

"I'm not. I'm telling you the truth."

The redhead turned to the smiling one, who was whispering something, and then turned back to her. "What about John Patrick? Do you know where we can find him?"

"No, I don't. Honest to God."

"You are lying again."

"I'm not! Maybe ask around the harbour in the city."

"Ask around the harbour in the city." He stared at her for a long time, as if tempted to do something and thinking about it. She saw it in his eyes. Unwavering, staring. So cold.

"I'm telling you the truth," she said again. "I don't know where John Patrick lives."

He moved, and for a moment she thought he might come into the kitchen, but then he didn't. He turned away and there was just the sound of the door opening and closing. She heard their footsteps on the stoop, then the car, tires crunching on the rock. The engine noise rising and fading away.

It took her a while to recover.

She lit a candle like her mother used to do against nightmares and misfortune and let it burn for a while. Then she blew out the flame and waved at the smoke.

At the sideboard in the living room she poured herself a small glass of blueberry wine. She sat in the green velour chair and looked out the window at the fog blowing in. She sipped the wine and when the glass was empty she poured another splash and sipped that too. Then she went back into the kitchen and called Franklin. She let it ring for a long time, then she hung up and looked for the inspector's card in the bowl on the credenza. She held it to the window light and reached for the telephone again. While it rang, she thought of that man's frozen smile. The flash of his teeth and the gun. Their spotless shined city shoes and the cuffs of their suit trousers, all so uncommonly neat.

Then someone answered the phone.

When Sully arrived he walked with her through the house. Upstairs they'd left some drawers half open, and in Danny's closet some of his clothes were on the floor.

She called him Sergeant and he called her Mrs. McInnis. They sat down at the kitchen table, and he took out a notebook and ballpoint pen and asked her to describe the men.

She would speak a tumbled sentence or two and he would slow her down and ask clarifying questions and then bend over his book and write. It took a long time. He wanted to know details of the men's clothing: what kinds of shined shoes? Smallish, narrow ones? What about their haircuts and expressions? And what about the smiling man's gun? Was it a revolver or a pistol?

He let her see his service pistol. Yes, maybe something like that, said Aileen. In a holster under his arm. Then the car. What make, model, licence plate? About that, Aileen had no idea.

"I never knew about cars," she said. "It looked new and shiny. You don't often see a car like that around here."

"Maybe it was a rental," said Sullivan. "If we sent a police artist, could you sit with her and describe the men and help her draw a likeness of them?"

"Surely," she said. "Yes, of course I can do that."

When Sully had left she tried Franklin again. This time he answered, and not long after that he came up to the house. He brought dinner, in two paper bags from the Swiss Chalet takeout. She went upstairs to change out of her housedress, and back in the kitchen she put the chicken quarters and the baked potatoes and coleslaw on her good china plates and set out cutlery and linen napkins. The sour cream she put on a little side plate and the sauce she poured from the waxed cardboard container into the gravy boat from her mother. She took two beers from the fridge and opened them and set them on the kitchen table along with two glasses. Her hands were still a bit unsteady.

He came down the stairs from the bathroom in his sock feet.

"You tidied up already," he said. "Upstairs. I would have helped you."

"It wasn't much."

"Wasn't it. But don't you think you should be calling Margaret again?"

"Not now, Franklin. Sit down. In the other chair, you like that better. And I just dragged Margaret out here for nothing and then sent her back home. I can't call her again."

"Yes, you can. And you know why. Because these were dangerous people. They know where you live and they were asking for Danny by name."

"I know that. Let's just eat now. Please."

They took up their cutlery and ate.

After a long while she said, "So good. Thank you, Franklin. So very good."

Later they sat in the parlour, she in the green velour chair, he on the couch. They talked about Danny and John Patrick. About the two men who had come looking for them. Franklin didn't know what to think of it all.

He said, "Maybe at least call Margaret and get her advice. Let her decide if she wants to come out. And does that mean that John Patrick and Danny are both using the same boat? Your boat."

"It's not my boat any more. I gave it to Danny."

"So is Danny lending it to him? For what? For something shady? Maybe tell the boy to keep away from him for a while. If people like that are looking for him."

"I can tell Danny what I want, and he'll do what he wants. What he thinks is right. He's a good boy."

"I'm not saying he isn't."

"Last time he was here he brought me this from the city." She opened her cardigan.

Franklin looked, but she could tell he didn't know what she meant.

"The blouse, Franklin! It's linen, and he knows I like those pale blues."

"Oh. Nice, Aillie. Real nice."

Late that night she woke when she heard a car on the rock. She got out of bed and looked down from the window. Her heart was hammering. So black down there, no moon, no stars. But it looked bigger than a car. Boxier. She hoped it was Danny's truck. She heard the front door. "Danny!"

she called. "Is that you?" She found her slippers under the bed and patted down her hair and went to her bedroom door. She opened it. "Danny, is that you?"

"Who else, Mom?" He was coming up the stairs in the dark.

She flicked on the light on the landing and he covered his eyes with his hand for a moment and put the hand down again. "Too bright, Mom. Don't. Go back to bed."

But she didn't turn the light off and she didn't go back to bed.

"Where have you been all this time?"

"Some of the south loop. There was wind damage in places and I had to take care of that."

"Two suspicious-looking men were here today, asking for you and John Patrick. What's that all about?"

"In what way suspicious?"

"One had a pistol under his coat."

"A pistol."

"And he never said a word, as if he didn't speak any English. And the other one never took no for an answer. Foreigners in coats and suits and city shoes like the one you found on the island."

She followed him into his room. "They looked in all the drawers. And through the clothes in your closet. What were they looking for?"

"How should I know? Did you call the police?"

"I did. Sully came and I made a report. They were asking for you and John Patrick by name. What's that all about, Danny?"

"I don't know. Did they say what they wanted?"

"They wanted you and John Patrick and the boat. Are you letting him use our boat?"

He had sat down on the bed. The quilt on it was the one she made for him when he was maybe ten years old.

"What did you tell them, Mom?"

"That I didn't know where you were and that I don't know where John Patrick lives. What's this all about, Danny? Look at me."

"They were probably more police. Plainclothes, from a different unit."

"I don't think so, and neither did Sully. They were asking where you're keeping the boat. I was thinking that maybe they went through your pockets to find a marina tag or something. Are you letting him use it?"

When he didn't answer, she sat down next to him on the bed. "Are you, Danny?"

"Mom. I'm really tired. Maybe they were just looking to get a ride somewhere."

"A ride somewhere? The way they were dressed? What kind of ride, where? And what's John Patrick got to do with all that?"

"I don't know. He is looking for a job, but no one's hiring him. He's a good skipper. Best I ever worked with."

"And?"

"And nothing. If I can help him out, I will."

"Could it have anything to do with those dead kids on the island, Danny? Could it be John Patrick had anything to do with it?"

He looked sideways at her. "Mom, what are you asking?"

"You heard me. Could it be?"

"No. Never. I have no idea what they wanted. There's crackpots out there, and if you reported it to the police then that's all we can do. And I'm really tired. Can we not do this now?"

"Crackpots is right. You be careful, Danny. Maybe stay away from John Patrick for a while until the police find out what's going on."

"Okay. Just stop it now." He stood up. "I need to go to the bathroom."

She watched him walk out of the room, and when she'd heard the bathroom door close she got down on both knees and raised the bedskirt and looked under the bed. But it was too dark in there to see much. She stood up.

"Night, Danny," she said on the landing.

—

She lay awake for a long time. Around two o'clock in the morning she felt her bedroom to be unbearably warm, and she got up and opened the window all the way and put her forehead to the fly screen. The smell of rust on the screen. Darkest night out there.

Back in bed she lay listening for cars coming down their road. *Don't*, she told herself. *Do not.*

She tried to listen only to the ocean and to the rocks speaking in the dark. Hear them rumble, Aillie, her father used to say. They're talking to each other. Telling wise old stories. Thousands of years old. Hear them? What are they saying, girl? Be very quiet inside and listen, and you'll know.

At one point she could hear the owl. Could hear its call and then hear the sound of its slow, powerful wing-beat among the trees of the night. All quiet then, save for the rocks.

Fifteen

THE POLICE ARTIST was a young woman in jeans and a denim jacket. With Aileen's help she worked quickly and well, at first with a kit and then refining the details. Before very long the drawings of the two men lay on the kitchen table and they all stood looking down at them.

"What do you think, Mrs. McInnis?" said Inspector Sorensen.

"They're very good. That smiling one especially. It's like I can remember him more than the other. But the other one is good too. He had reddish hair. The noses and eyes are good. The chins. They're good pictures."

"All right. Thank you. Danny, have you ever seen these two?"

"I can't say I have."

"Take a good long look."

"I don't think so. Honestly."

"You don't think so," said Sorensen. "Have you or haven't you seen them? I need a firm yes or no. They came to this house asking for you by name."

Danny leaned over the table. It was very quiet in the kitchen. He studied the pictures for a while longer. He looked pale and nervous to Aileen. Not himself.

He shook his head. "No, I haven't."

"Are you sure?"

"Why do you keep asking the boy that same question?" said Aileen. "Over and over. When he's told you five times already that no, he hasn't seen them."

Sorensen ignored her. "Are you, Danny? Sure?"

"Yes, I am sure. I've never seen them before."

"Are you in contact with John Patrick Croft? Do you have any dealings with him?"

"Hardly any."

"Hardly any. Meaning some?"

"Well, I did want to help him out. We're friends, and I got a boat and paying work, and he doesn't right now."

"So are you in fact helping him out?"

"Well, yes. Maybe I am."

"Maybe you are. Helping him out how?"

"Inspector, you're putt'n too much pressure on the boy!" said Aileen, angrily now. "Danny, you don't have to say anything if you don't want to. I think I'll call Margaret again, and you don't say anything until she's here."

"Mom! For heaven's sake. You aren't doing me any favours here. I can do this on my own. And yes, I did let John Patrick use the boat to do a few island properties for me while I did some on land in the truck. And I gave him half my fee. It saves me time, with the storms coming any day now."

There was a silence, and then the inspector said, "Very interesting, that. We'll need a list of the properties John Patrick did for you. And I'll ask you for the last time now, do you have any idea what those men might have wanted from the two of you? What they might have been looking for. Here, in your mother's house."

"None. No idea. I'm telling you."

"Have you ever been approached by someone to do a quick run in the dark for them? A little pick-up? What's the fee for that now, around three thousand?"

"No. Never. I don't know what you're talking about."

Sorensen studied him, taking his time.

"Of course you know what I'm talking about, Danny. Has John Patrick Croft been approached, you think? We'll be asking him. What do you think he'll say?"

"About what?"

Sorensen was still watching him. No emotion to the

man, she thought. Just this cold thinking, analysing his hunches. Keeping mental notes.

Eventually he said, "All right. I'll let it go for now, Danny. But we're nowhere near done with this."

When Sorensen and the artist had left, but their presence like some afterimage was still in the room, Aileen said, "That man is hard as nails, and he suspects something and he won't let go. Danny, this is very serious now. What's he saying, stuff that he thinks you know something about? And approached about what?"

Danny shook his head. He said nothing, just sat at the table looking down at his hands, and she saw him, his tousled hair, a grown man's face and shoulders now but her little boy still there, like now, around his eyes, squinting at some thoughts he didn't like, didn't want to let in.

"We need to be smart here, Danny. And just so you know it, I will be calling Margaret again. And this time we better show some gratitude. You hear me? We have no idea what's going on here and we need help. *You* need help. Okay?"

And after a while he looked up at her and nodded okay.

THE DEAL

Sixteen

BY THE END of the next day Margaret was back in Sweetbarry. She'd told Hugh briefly what it was all about, and that this was very important to her. She promised that she wouldn't neglect her work in the least. She would take the files with her and this time also the out-of-office pager so he'd be able to reach her any time, day or night. She'd called him Hughie, which in the right mood he liked, and it mellowed him.

He had looked at her across his desk and seen something in her face and eyes, and he'd sighed and sunk down a bit in his chair. He'd argued a bit, not very much, and in the end he'd agreed.

Now, in stiff old workboots and her father's canvas coverall, she paced off the distance from the phone terminal on the outside gable wall of the house to the boathouse and added a few yards. From repairs some years ago there was a length of black phone wire left on a spool in the workroom. She rolled it out, and there was enough of it to go through the boathouse wall to the oak desk by the window. She stripped the wire ends with a paring knife and then drove to Telford Herman's boatyard and told him what she intended to do. Telford listened, then he gave her a hand drill and a three-eighths-of-an-inch auger bit, and to seal the hole in the wall around the wire he gave her a few small wooden wedges and some caulking putty in a tin.

At the second-hand shop behind the co-op she found a push-button phone, an extension cord with the jack box still on it, and a desk lamp. Back home she installed the box and the telephone line and connected the line at both ends. The answering machine she left hooked up in the kitchen.

She scrubbed and polished the desk and oiled the squeak in the spring hinge of the oaken chair, and she cleaned the window with vinegar and water and newspaper. She emptied the desk drawers and set the phone ringer at half volume, and from that phone called her pager. It all worked.

She called their number at the house in Toronto and let it ring, and when the machine picked up she said she'd been home for a few days but now was back in Sweetbarry. Call me, she said to him.

———

The police diver arrived in a van with the logo of a diving school, and because Aileen's rock already had two cars and a truck on it, he parked in Margaret's drive and walked up to knock on Aileen's door. He was a young man in faded jeans and running shoes. He said *sir* to the inspector and *ma'am* to Aileen and her.

She wanted to come along again, but the inspector did not allow it. He said it was a diving run and had nothing to do with Danny. In any case, they could talk later.

As Danny told it afterward, they tied up again at the dock and then the diver put on his wetsuit and mask and flippers and made his first dive. He came up once for air, and the second time when he surfaced he held up an open folding knife and he reached and slapped it wetly on the dock. He went down again. On this dive he came up for air twice, and the third time he held up two brass cartridge shells. At the stern ladder he passed them to the inspector and climbed back into the boat.

———

She and Sorensen stood by his car on the rock in the last sunlight coming down between the trees.

"I have a favour to ask," he said.

"A favour? All right, let's hear it."

"I'll give you a bit of background first. We now know more about how the kids died. As I suspected, the blood on the dock isn't just from them. The large, heavy stain with the shoe print in it is from a third person. None of the kids bled that much, and there are signs of arterial spray and then heavy flow. So let's say for now that the boy stood in front of the girl and fought back or attacked someone with a knife. There was some sort of violent struggle and then the boy was shot."

"And the girl with him?"

"Yes. We know that for a fact. From their hands, they weren't working class. Pen bunions on their right middle fingers suggest they were used to writing. Perhaps students. Perhaps girlfriend and boyfriend, but we don't know. All of this may mean very little, but it does narrow the field."

"What were they doing out there?"

"We don't know that either. I have my suspicions, but that's all they are for now. The police artist has already made pictures of them as they would have looked alive, and those pictures are in wide circulation."

"Can I have copies? I want to post them at the community hall. Someone may have seen them."

"Yes. I'll have copies sent to you. Along with pictures of the men."

"Thank you. So what's the favour?"

"It has to do with the blood on the dock. The arterial spray and the heavy flow. I'm sure Danny will tell you that we found a knife, and so that is of course a clue, and whoever lost all that blood is either dead or has found help with some private doctor or in a hospital. We've sent telexes to the hospitals in the area, but so far there's been no response. Many hospitals report gunshot wounds voluntarily, to protect themselves in case of a crime, but with anything else they're reluctant to have the police poke around. I know that Mrs. McInnis still works as a nurse, and I'm wondering if she would help us with this. Would you mind asking her? Massive blood loss from some traumatic injury, perhaps to the left side of the body. A deep slash across an artery, I'd say. It's probably registered as an accident."

"Shouldn't that request be coming from you?"

"I don't think so. Not directly. It's a bit tricky. Mrs. McInnis doesn't exactly like me, and it'll require a fair bit of goodwill on her part because she'll have to be asking around among her colleagues. And hospital policies and politics being what they are—you know what I'm saying. It might take a bit of persuasion, but as their lawyer you can tell her that finding the hospital will help the case. And it will."

"You want her to find out from emergency room nurses if there were any admissions with significant blood loss?"

"Yes. Even more than significant. Life-threatening. Near-catastrophic, I'd say."

She studied him for a moment.

"All right," she said then. "I'll do it. If we're successful, there will be a favour that I'm going to ask from you in return. One favour for another. A sort of deal."

He nodded. "Depends on the favour. But fair enough."

When his car had disappeared up the gravel road, she climbed the stoop to Aileen's house and opened the door and went inside.

"Life-threatening blood loss," said Aileen when Margaret had told her what the inspector wanted. "Is that it?"

"Yes. *Near-catastrophic* was the way he put it. Maybe the left side of the body and probably through an artery."

"They won't be allowed to talk about that. Or want to. There's strict hospital policies."

"He's aware of that. The point is that maybe they'll talk to you, being another nurse, and to help you out. I think you should try. I think we should do everything we can to help the police clear up this case."

—

At the boatyard she parked the Buick and took the hand drill and the tin of putty she'd come to return from the passenger seat. Telford Herman was busy working on a hull on the cradle.

"You're caulking this one, Telford?"

"We are, yes. She's still got a wooden hull, not fibre-glass." He ran his hand over the boards. "We do her every other year or so. This time we'll be replacing her bow piece too. She's got rot in hers." He took two steps and ran his hand down the bow curve.

"Are you using tamarack for that? I just read about that in a book on trees and the uses of wood. I found it in my father's workshop. And some of his notes on the planting."

He gave her a surprised look. "Tamarack, yes. That's the right wood for the bow piece. It's expensive, but at least you can find it again these days. When I was a young lad and my father ran this shop, you couldn't get any tama-rack, not for love or money. All gone. And most of the pines, Norway and white, them too. The British clear-cutting did most of the damage, and then our own lumber mills did the rest. Your father pedalled his bike all over the county, making his secret maps. An old mailman's bicycle he had. But you'll know all that."

"Actually, no, I don't. Not in any detail. When was that?"

"Oh. In the summers and falls when he was still at university, up in Wolfville. Before he married your mother. Using his survey maps to go all over and finding the last saplings of them, seedlings, and not telling anyone. He knew more about trees than any other man. Taught my own dad about winter buds.

"After that he started with all that soil, trucks full of soil going through town, I don't know how many truckloads. He got them for free from the gravel pit, topsoil, when they were expanding it. People thought he was a bit unusual, Charles. You know. Different. Setting his sight on things and doing them no matter what. Dogged. And his mother, your Grandmother AJ, she was unusual too. I guess that's where he got the bees in his bonnet from."

"It was eighty-eight truckloads, Telford," she said. "I read it in his notes."

She was close to tears and didn't know why. And Telford Herman, he could tell, because he looked away for a moment and then back at her, and kindly he said, "Well, yes, Margaret. Yes. Why don't you come and see us sometime? Come to the house and have tea with Mrs. Herman. She'd like that."

That night in dreams she prepared a birthing bed in the forest. Slim branches of spruce and hemlock on the ground and balsam fir and dried moss on top for softness. Walls of falling leaves and tamarack needles like bead curtains. For the newborn to come, she made a small crib of bent branches of red spruce and willow withes, and she lined it with cushions of moss and the finest new growth of balsam.

She placed the crib next to the bed and then sat down by her rock to wait for the first sign of pink to the east.

When she woke she could at first not remember the dream, but it came to her in fragments while she was in the kitchen making coffee. In her nightgown and robe she stepped into her boots and out the screen door and walked to the water, sipping from her cup. She stood on the rock shelf where she'd sat in her dream and looked out. The sun was just clear of the horizon, still compressed into an ellipsis, and she stood in its long light and closed her eyes and felt complete and at peace for this moment, for the first time in many months.

She took a deep breath and let it out slowly, and another. After a while she opened her eyes.

Thank you, she said.

Going back up to the house she touched the tamarack with its soft needles turning yellow. Up high on the white spruce the cones were losing their green now. Beads of resin sparkling orange in the morning sun.

She dressed in a good dark-grey skirt and white blouse and jacket to go to her desk in the boathouse because it helped her frame of mind, and then she spent most of that day at her desk and on the telephone. She spoke with Jenny about the new files and arranged to have certain pages copied and couriered to her. There was a new corporation transfer, this one for a Hong Kong client who worked through an office in London. And there was a new client in New York.

She ate lunch in her kitchen and by two o'clock she was back at work. To her right, the blackboard where she'd developed her diagrams of legal order, her first ideas of abstraction as a student, was still bolted to the wall and bits of chalk lay on the sill. The connectedness of the threads of the intentions of the law, spirit and practice, all forms and branches of law into the order of a fabric designed for the upholding of specific rules of human interaction. In the early years she had believed fervently in all that.

Once, in her last year at Osgoode Hall, she'd demonstrated her idea in front of the class, and there had been only silence and doubtful looks, but afterward the professor had called her to his office and invited her to talk a bit more about it. He made notes as she spoke. Really? he said every so often. Go on, Miss Joubert.

Seventeen

EVERY MORNING SHE STILL took the wedding ring from the bathroom vanity and put it on her finger and turned it in the light. The traditional left ring finger, as they'd agreed back then, even though the right finger had been fashionable for a while in the fifties. But they would be hard-working professionals with busy right hands. Both with their brand new degrees, his in geology, hers in law, and her early interest in law mostly because Grandmother had instilled in her the old-world belief that law was about justice and as a result it was the noblest of professions.

Fresh out of law school in Toronto, she'd applied for an articling position at two different law firms, and was told there were no openings. Eventually she landed a job with a firm on Danforth Avenue. They paid her next to nothing and used her mostly as a filing clerk and to make coffee and fetch lunch at the corner. The lawyers, all men, winked at her and invited her for drinks.

She stuck it out until the bar exam, hoping the firm would give her real work then, and pay more. They did not, and so she found other jobs. One of them she walked out of when, after hours, a junior lawyer cornered her against the telex machine. She struggled, and it helped greatly that the machine suddenly began to chatter and type.

She found another job in an office on Bathurst Street, and this one lasted long enough for her to meet her articling requirements. Two months before Andrew was born, they let her go because they were worried about the demands of motherhood.

She loved her time with baby Andrew—the nursing, the sweetness of it all, the closeness. But at the same time, if she was honest, she often also wearied of it. In those moods she wanted her body back. All this nursing on demand, for hours. She missed getting out, missed the challenge of work, missed her independence, and at the same time felt guilty feeling that way. She admitted it only to Aileen on the phone. With Aileen she could talk about it, and because of little Danny, who was only a year and a half older, Aileen understood exactly.

Meanwhile Jack was brilliantly successful, and it had become clear to her that Canada with its resource-based economy had a far greater need for keen new exploration geologists than it had for keen new women lawyers. It seemed Jack could spot good properties by knowing almost intuitively what the geological ages and the ice ages had done in certain geographies, how strata in others had risen up and broken apart to mirror certain events at depth, and how to run the geophysics and plan his core samples. With skill and youthful enthusiasm he quickly became a sought-after mine-finder, and often he was gone three, four weeks at a time, travelling all over the world. He was gone more than he was home.

By the time she was ready to go back to work, she had a gap in her resumé, still no courtroom experience, and the responsibility of a child at home. She did find new jobs, usually short-term replacement jobs, and to be able to leave the house she had a series of live-in and day nannies. Because she'd read up on the benefits of breast milk over formula, she pumped milk and put it in small jars with the date and hour on them. She kept a second pump in a locked desk drawer at the office for emergencies, and often when she had to work late, or when the nanny called in a panic, she'd pump in the washroom at the office and send the jars wrapped in wet papers and plastic home in a taxi.

It was true what she'd told Michael about the teasing and insults from her colleagues in those early days. What she'd never talked about to anyone except Aileen, never to Michael or Jack, was the shame of it. The shame for herself, and even more so her shame and contempt for the men, who always only grinned at her and winked, as though the cracks about full-fat milk and milkmaids in her condition were some sort of clever mating call.

After a while she learned to smile and stare them down until their grins froze on their faces. The decision she made, and confirmed over and over in the private stillness of some taxi going home late at night, was that this was all just part of the price of admission. It was something unpleasant to be endured, and surely before long to be left behind.

As it happened, it was in corporate work where eventually she found her niche. The firm she worked for at the time took on a complicated tax case, and the lawyer told her to learn the file by heart and then to find whatever supportive material she could and brief him.

She spent days and nights at it and built a file for him of similar cases and their rulings, each case with an outline of fact, principle, and procedure, and in the end it all worked out exceptionally well. She did more cases for that same lawyer, all white-collar crime and tax issues, and after a while he took her with him to court and introduced her as his associate counsel.

Soon other lawyers noticed her, and after all the rejection and condescension early on she eventually received good offers from other law firms. From then on, she was on her way. She made tax loopholes, tax deferral, and tax jurisdictions her first specialty, and after a while added investment law and offshore ownership. In time she became very good at it all, and she was proud of that fact. It gave her confidence. She told herself that this was her gift, the gift to organize her life around, and she treated it with great respect. A solid career, and now, after many difficult years, nothing less than the promise of a partnership at a top law firm with international clients and multi-million-dollar cases.

In the evening Aileen and Franklin saw the small beam of the flashlight in the dark, stopping and pointing up trees and moving on, the pale robe at times, and at times also a small gleam or reflection on Margaret's face.

"What's she got on?" said Franklin. "Glasses or something?"

"Safety glasses," said Aileen. "She told me. She's wearing them against the branches in the dark."

"But why? I mean, what's she doing out there?"

"She told me and I sort of understand, but it's hard to explain."

"Try me."

"You'll think it's weird."

"What if I don't?"

"She's going back a while. The other day she started look-ing for a book about trees she remembered, a children's story. And the thing is, I remember it too. Trees talking to each other. The love and kindness among them, their roots all in the same soil. Don't smirk, or I'll stop telling you anything any more this minute."

"No, no. Go on."

"It came from England, kind of like the Curious George book. It was sweet and it was a popular book in our days. She was looking in her dad's work shed at the back of the boathouse, and that's where she found the safety glasses and his ring binders with notes about the forest and a textbook on trees and lumber."

"Charles's notes? When he did all that planting?"

"Yes. Eighty-eight truckloads of soil, it says in the notes. She told me. He made notes on all the native trees he planted there, the ones he wanted to preserve after some of them were practically wiped out by the shipbuilding. Bicycling all over and scratching around for seedlings, he was, among deadfall in the clear-cuts."

"And why is she out there now? In the dark?"

"Probably because she can't sleep. Why else? And she's working things out."

"What things?"

"Just things, Franklin."

They watched from the picture window, leaning forward to see Margaret's little light winking and moving and pausing among the trees, heading back up the slope to her house now.

"She might trip out there," he said. "And she might drive off the fox."

"No, she won't drive off the fox. She likes it here, and she trusts us by now. The fox does. I heard her tonight before you came up. And all those cars today were an exception too. I think she knows that."

"The fox knows that?"

"Yes."

"Don't you go soft on me too now, Aillie."

"I'm doing nothing of the kind. And neither is Margaret. She's planning to identify all her trees. Put little labels on them. She says creating order calms her."

When Franklin left she watched him from the window in the half-dark. His bright windbreaker, his unruly white hair, heading for the path down to his place. He was carrying a flashlight because he'd fallen on these rocks more than once already and he had a bad knee.

When she couldn't see him any more she turned into the room and picked up the glasses and carried them into the kitchen. Out the window her old Vauxhall was the only car on the rock. Danny was away in his truck, on his south loop again.

She tidied the kitchen and turned out the light and headed up the narrow stairs to her bedroom. She thought of Grandmother Dotty in her wooden shoes clomping up and down here. Danny once said it was like living inside a guitar, especially once the fall wires were up.

She opened her bedroom door and in the dark stepped around the bed to the window and opened it wide to the night air and all the sounds she loved.

Eighteen

THE POLICE DRAWINGS of the two men and the dead young people arrived by courier. Margaret signed for the package and slit it open and put the pictures on the kitchen table. There were several copies of each, all pasted to art board trimmed to size. The images were very good. She telephoned Aileen to come and see them.

"This one here," said Aileen. "The smiling one, it's so good it could be from a photograph. His pinched lips. And the eyes on both of them. Still gives me the creeps. And the kids, dear God. She's beautiful. And the boy looks sweet."

An hour later, Margaret put the pictures on the passenger seat and drove along the shore road to the church. The sun was going down behind the town, dark red dipping into a cloudbank, red in the sky and the edges of the clouds golden. Two ospreys circled motionless in some high vector like hands on a clock, the white and grey on their heads and chests bright orange in the setting sun.

She parked on the church lot and then crossed the wooden bridge to the rock. Inside St. Peter's she walked down the centre aisle and around the altar and past the vestry to the small office Reverend McMurtry kept there.

When she heard a typewriter she hesitated for a moment, then she knocked. The typing stopped.

"Come in," said his strong voice.

He sat at his desk, turned sideways to face the typewriter on the pull-out tablet. He put on his glasses and stood up. "Mrs. Bradley. Margaret." He walked around his desk and offered his hand. He pointed at the wooden chair in front of his desk and swung another one in from the wall.

"What can I do for you?"

She passed him the sketches of the children. "I imagine you've heard about them, Reverend. They were found dead under the dock at Crieff Island."

"Yes, I've heard. Sergeant Sullivan and a detective were here, and they showed me the forensic pictures. Not these." He sat looking down at the images and shook his head. "Terrible."

"Isn't it. Reverend, I'm wondering if we could post the pictures in the church notice box. In case someone saw them."

"Yes, of course we can do that. And what about the notice box at AJ Hall?"

"Well, there I'll be posting the pictures of the men who may have murdered them. I don't want them side by side in the same window."

"No," he said.

He looked down at the pictures. The celluloid in his collar was the whitest thing in the room.

"And there's something else, Reverend."

"Yes?"

"I would very much like to have a funeral service for them here in our church. And a burial in our churchyard."

He sat back in the chair and looked at her.

"They died in our community," she said.

"I know. But a funeral, here. And we don't even know who they are. Or where they're from. Have the bodies been released by the authorities?"

"I don't know. Is that a yes?"

"No, it's not a yes, Margaret. I need to think about it. A funeral service and a burial is no small matter. Also, there have to be parents somewhere."

"That's what the police are trying to find out. These pictures are in wide circulation now. I'm asking in case the parents can't be found."

"So let's wait. Rather than make hasty decisions about

funerals. In the meantime I'll post these in the notice box. And I'll mention them in the announcement part of our Sunday service."

On the way back she stopped at AJ Hall and let herself in with her key. In the office she sat at the desk and hand-printed a note:

URGENT!

HAVE YOU SEEN THESE MEN?

IF SO, PLEASE TELL SERGEANT SULLIVAN.

She closed up the office and walked out into the hall-way, and in the notice box pinned up the pictures side by side and her note underneath them.

When she drove home it was nearly night. At the turnoff to her house she saw the eyes of the vixen and her two cubs bright green in the headlights. She stopped the car and switched off the lights and the engine. When her eyes had adjusted she could see the outlines of them against the brighter rock. The mother was standing absolutely still with one front paw raised, watching the car, the cubs crowding her. Then the mother set down the paw and nosed them along, and soon they were gone among the bushes.

—

That day Aileen had found a nurse who was willing to talk to them about a serious blood loss case, and in the morning they drove into the city to show her the pictures. Aileen sat in the passenger seat, not in jeans or cords this time, but in a print dress and leather shoes and a fall coat, with her good purse in her lap.

In places there was dense fog again, and Margaret slowed down and switched on her low beams and the flashers. Then the fog lifted and the sun came out. Leaves were turning everywhere. Bright gold on the birches, deep orange and wine-red on the maples.

"She doesn't want me to tell you her name," said Aileen. "And I promised no names of the doctors either, okay? Remember that. I know all about the nasty politics in a hospital. She and I pulled many shifts together, in Emergency quite often, and when Clearwater closed she got hired in the city and moved there. She's younger than I."

In the city they waited in the parking lot by the hospital side entrance until the nurse came out and saw them. Aileen introduced Margaret and then moved to the back seat.

The nurse seemed nervous. She pointed to the far corner of the parking lot. "Let's go over there, can we? And I have only a few minutes because my break is almost over." She turned in the seat and said to Aileen, "I shouldn't be doing this at all, but I told you I would, and so here I am. How are you, Aileen?"

"I'm all right, thanks. I could use more shifts, but I'm gett'n by. And you?"

"So-so. Fine. How is your boy?"

"He's doing well. He's got the boat and he's making good use of it. But now this strange thing, the dead kids and these scary men."

"I know. Times are changing, Aileen. It used to be we knew every last person around here. Not any more."

When the car was stopped again Aileen handed the sketches forward, and the nurse took them and studied them.

"This one," she said.

"The smiling one," Margaret said to Aileen in the back seat. To the nurse she said, "You're sure? Excuse the question, but are you?"

"Oh, I'm sure. I was in Emergency when they came in. I think it was the other one that brought him. Kind of reddish hair?"

"Yes."

"They spoke Spanish with each other. The injured one was white as a sheet. The one who brought him in said they'd been out on a fishing boat as paying tourists and his friend tripped and gashed himself on some equipment. We've seen some of those injuries and it could have been, and so we didn't ask too many questions. They weren't exactly dressed for on the water and they couldn't remember the name of the boat, but with foreign tourists you never know."

"So you checked him in," said Margaret.

"We did. He had one long, deep gash in his left arm. Bad, but with a tight tourniquet on it, made from his shirt sleeve. The first thing they did was clamp him and give him blood. I don't know how many units. Then they wheeled him into the operating room."

"For how long was he in the hospital?" said Margaret.

"Not very long. Four, five days. Must have been a good healer. When he checked out, the friend brought clothes, and when he was dressed they put his arm in a sling. The friend paid cash in American dollars."

"When he came in, was he wearing both shoes?" said Margaret.

"No, he wasn't," said the nurse. "Now that you mention it. But that's not unusual in a trauma case. A missing shoe is nothing. In a car crash they lose their watches. Rings. Their teeth. And this was just a loafer." She looked out the window and across the parking lot. "I should be going."

"A *loafer*," said Margaret. "Was it a pretty fancy loafer?"

"It was soaking wet. All his clothes were."

"Just the shoe," said Margaret. "Was it the right shoe he had on, and did it have a yellow metal bangle across the instep?"

"I don't know about right or left. And a bangle. I can't . . ." The nurse looked around out the windows. "I should go."

"Just this last question, please."

"Well, I think maybe it did have a metal bangle. The shoe came off when they put him on the gurney and I picked it up and put it beside him."

On the way back to Sweetbarry, Aileen said, "Maybe that's why he kept his left hand in his coat pocket the whole time. A sling would have been too noticeable, so he used the pocket for support. What are we going to tell the inspector? I don't want her to get into any kind of trouble."

"She won't. When the police come and ask questions they can say they're following up on the telexes to hospitals. So this one won't feel singled out. I'll mention all that to the inspector when I call him. But anyway, I don't think they did anything illegal. An accident on a fishing boat would have sounded quite plausible."

—

Later that day she called Sorensen from the telephone in the boathouse.

"I can now tell you that we found the hospital where the smiling man was treated for a life-threatening gash in his left arm."

"Can you! Where?"

"Remember our deal? I said I might want to ask a favour in return."

"Yes. And I said it depends on the favour."

"I want the bodies of the two young people released into my care, and I'll look after them and get them a proper funeral here in Sweetbarry."

There was a silence.

"Released to you. Are you sure?"

"Yes. Someone needs to take care of them."

"We're still searching for the parents."

"I'm saying if you can't find them."

"It's a bit unusual, but I can put in the request. I can't make any promises."

"The request is all I'm asking for."

"There'll be forms to fill out and sign. With unclaimed bodies, disposal is usually done without fuss through the morgue. Are you really sure about this?"

"Yes, I'm sure."

"All right. So tell me what you found out."

———

That evening she tried to reach Jack. She called him from the kitchen phone. She dialled the number twice, but each time there was only the answering machine with her own voice on the tape. You have reached the home of Mr. and Mrs. Bradley . . .

The second time, she left a message asking him to call back because she did want him to know that something had changed within her. Like a door opening. A way forward.

In cooler moments she could see it to be unusual, an attempt to rewrite laws writ in blood at the very dawn of life, but in moments like now, in this nighttime kitchen in this old wooden house, it seemed wonderful and so very plausible, and not in any need of explanation.

What she wanted was to be entrusted with these children. To make them hers and to be allowed to do the right thing by them. The right thing this time, since these would be the last children she would ever be entrusted with. Having somehow lost all her others.

She picked up the phone again and hung it up. There was no reason to think he was home, but it was possible. Or he might be on his way home. She waited for a long time for him to call back that night, but he never did.

Nineteen

WHILE SHE WAITED and hoped to hear from Jack and Reverend McMurtry and Sorensen, she worked on her files, had tea with Mrs. Herman, and helped Aileen and Franklin make wine. Waiting and hoping was not something she was good at.

"The women of my mother's generation," Grandmother had once said to her, "and even of mine, too many of them, that's all they ever did. Wait and hope for a man to come and change their lives for them. And then get bitter and blame everyone else if it didn't happen. I never believed in that, and don't you either, Margaret."

But now there was no choice other than to wait and hope, and the winemaking helped. They used the mash with the skins, and sugar and some of last year's wine as a starter, then they covered the fermenting jars with tea towels and set them down out of the way in a corner in the parlour. Once in a while Aileen would have to remove the covers and push the risen heads back down with the masher. In a few days, if the alcohol content needed boosting, they'd add sugar to feed the yeast some more.

And one afternoon, sitting with Mrs. Herman in her parlour with the sun on the rose wallpaper, Margaret talked about one of Andrew's last summers out here, when she and Jack had nearly three weeks off at the same time, which was rare, and Andrew could get ten days' leave. They took a cruise on a schooner north around Cape Breton and back down and south through the Strait of Canso, past Port Hastings and Mulgrave. Sleeping in narrow berths, just the three of them and another couple and a small crew. All the amazing wildlife, seals on the rocks at Cape North, whales blowing. Jack and Andrew and she had spent hours looking out, sun-warm and happy the three of them. Pointing things out to each other. Look! Look! The little puffins that seemed to be moving through water with the same short wingbeats that they used to move through air. They ate meals on deck and talked and laughed.

"I think the schooner was the *Annabelle*," she said to Mrs. Herman. "Out of Halifax."

Mrs. Herman, who was a bit hard of hearing, smiled and nodded.

That cruise had been one of the last things they'd done as a family. There was a photograph of the three of them on her dresser, arms around one another's shoulders, the boy between them, Jack and Andrew unshaven, everyone grinning.

Late on Sunday Jack finally did call. He said he'd just come from the airport and picked up her messages. There'd been a delay, he said. The mine owners were unhappy with the assay results, and additional test drills would be necessary. He sounded tired.

"How are you, Margaret?"

She said she was fine, mostly. Better, out here. She told him about the men who'd come to see Aileen, about the pictures of the men and the children, and that they'd found the hospital where the wounded man had been treated.

"So much going on," he said.

"I'm also at my desk eight hours a day."

She told him she was planning a funeral for the children.

"A funeral? Who are these kids?"

"The police are trying to find that out."

She waited, and into his silence she said, "Could you come out for that, Jack? For the funeral."

"Are you serious?"

"Well . . . yes."

"I'm surprised, Margaret. The last time we spoke you didn't want me to stay because you needed time."

"I know. But would you come out?"

"Honestly? No, Margaret. I wouldn't want to. It's also very busy right now because metals are up everywhere. Especially silver."

"Is it."

"And I'll probably also have to go back to British Columbia soon. So the answer is no, Margaret. Sorry. What else is going on?"

The next day Inspector Sorensen paid her a surprise visit. There were strong winds and rain, and he parked his car and hurried up to the house.

"Wild weather down here," he said. He took off his hat but kept on the coat. They stood in her little hall by the front door.

"What's the verdict?" she said. "Any news on our deal?"

"Yes, in a way."

"So come and sit down."

He took off his coat and hung it on a peg and put the hat over it. They sat at the kitchen table and she put out some red pepper cornbread and butter and olives and turned on the kettle.

He told her that because the opinion at forensics was that the young people were Latin American, he had widened the search with pictures by police wire into Mexico and further south.

"They were about twenty and twenty-two years old," he said. "The boy was the older."

"And?"

"And, well, here it comes. I believe they were couriers. Cocaine, most likely. It all fits a pattern that we're seeing more and more, and the profile is right too because it's often the children of the upper middle class. You know, sheltered lives, young and easy to talk into a short adventure, and no one would suspect them. The parents have no idea, of course.

"They come on airplanes and sometimes on ships, mostly up from Mexico. Compared to the States, our coastline is wide open and customs at our airports is very tourist-friendly. Kids bring it in, like on a little holiday, a lark, but for very good money. They are met by contacts like the two men who came to Aileen's house, and the contacts feed the product into distribution, often south into the States.

"I'm in charge of this coastline down to Yarmouth, so I know a little bit about it. So far it's only cocaine. You know, body belts and vests and plastic bags of it folded in clothing in suitcases. But then there are also the drops from freighters and the nighttime pickups of much larger amounts, for which they use local fishermen, who know these waters well. We don't know as yet exactly how the transfers work, or how the kids ended up on that island."

"If they were only couriers, why were they killed?"

"We don't know that either. For one thing, they were disposable. Perhaps there was a problem with money. But more likely they saw or heard something they shouldn't have and so became a liability. I think the boy fought them off or attacked them, and in the struggle both were killed."

He sat looking at her. "I wanted you to have the facts, in view of your funeral plans."

"Thank you. It's very sad."

The kettle whistled and she spooned instant coffee into two cups and poured water. She pushed cream and sugar his way.

"My grandmother remembered when you could buy coca powder in penny sachets in any drugstore as a little pick-me-up and a cure for headaches," she said. "Then it was criminalized and suddenly there was big money in it. But this changes nothing. If the parents can't be found I still want to look after them and arrange a funeral here. Did you file the request for them to be released to me?"

"I did. Someone from the morgue will call you one way or another."

"Thank you. What about the two men? Any news on them?"

"No, nothing. We've spoken to the hospital and sent blood samples to the forensic lab in Ottawa. The results are positive for a match with the blood on the dock. Something went badly wrong here, and either they set up another run or, more likely, they've disappeared. Gone home and been replaced by others. But we're still watching the borders and airports, and their pictures are everywhere."

He picked up a fork and speared an olive. "Nice. I like them like this, soft and without the pits." He took a sip of coffee, reached for a slice of cornbread, bit into it and chewed. "Very good. What are the little red bits in it?"

"Red pepper. How long before they decide about releasing the kids?"

"I can't say. Not that long. Days, not weeks."

Before he left she scooped the black olives back into the little container and snapped it shut. She wrapped a plastic fork in a paper napkin, put all that into a brown paper lunch bag together with some of the cornbread, and handed it to him.

"For the road," she said.

Twenty

IN HER LIVING ROOM Aileen lifted the covers on the wine jars and pushed down the heads. She could smell the fermentation working. She put on additional towels to keep the jars warm while she opened the seaside window to let out the fumes.

Later Franklin came up with the alcohol gauge, and he squeezed the bulb and lifted some of the wine and looked at the bubble. "Only three per cent," he said. "I think we should add sugar. Lots of it. And in a few days' time, if that doesn't do it we can pitch in some vodka."

He was at the sink rinsing the gauge, and as she passed him she clapped him on the back of his head.

"No, we won't. Not in *my* wine. And what's the rush? Three per cent after just a few days is a good start."

She went to the fridge and fetched him a beer. They

sat in the kitchen because she had closed the windows and the fumes in the parlour were strong.

"Margaret was here. That policeman came to see her."

She told him what Margaret had said.

"But she still wants a funeral for them?"

Aileen nodded.

"Can you explain that to me?"

"Explain what, Franklin? They're still just someone's children, far from home."

He frowned and then for a while he sipped his beer in silence.

"It's gett'n dark earlier now," he said. He looked at his watch.

"It is. And she's changed her hour with it. Coming a bit earlier now."

"Is she. So let's wait for her."

"They were probably students, Margaret says. The kids. She was the younger and he was looking out for her. Protecting her. Maybe because he got her into all this. And now Margaret is back to wanting to talk to the pathologist and to see them at the morgue. This time I gave in and said I'd call Barbie and she'll set it up."

She almost went on to explain why Margaret was doing all this, but then she didn't say anything. She knew Franklin would look at her sideways and ask questions, and she'd try and make him understand, but it was complicated. It was also not her business to explain Margaret to anyone.

He said, "Who do you think took them over to that island? The kids, in a boat."

"Could have been anyone along here. Anyone."

"You don't think it was maybe John Patrick in Danny's boat, do you? Because what are the chances of these two shooters coming here asking for them by name?"

"In Danny's boat . . . no, I don't think that. And don't you think it either. Such nonsense. Be quiet now, Franklin. Let's just sit and listen for her. You want the light on?"

"No."

And so they sat in the dark in silence for a while in the old house, waiting for the fox. He sipping his beer, she empty-handed. But she was upset now.

"Danny is in the clear," she said. "He has never even seen those men."

"All right, all right. Sorry. You know he does lend the boat to John Patrick. He said so himself. I was just think-ing out loud."

"Then don't you be doing that. Not about stuff like that. If word gets out about your loud thoughts."

"All right. All right. Sorry."

They sat waiting. They could hear the water and the rocks. The screen door banging over at Margaret's house.

"But if the boy is in the clear like you say, then why is she still here? Why hasn't she gone back to her job in Toronto by now?"

"Because she likes it here, and to arrange the funeral. She said if possible she might stay here until Thanksgiving. I know she's working in that boathouse all the time. I see the courier coming and going, and she's got a heater in there and a typewriter too now, and the phone. And there's the telex at the post office. So will you finally stop talking? You want another beer?"

"No, thanks, Aileen. I'm fine."

Danny did come home that night, but not until three in the morning. She heard the truck and then the front door, and when he came up in his sock feet she stood on the landing in her nightgown and clicked on the light.

"Where you been, Danny? Do you know what time it is?"

He stood shielding his eyes. "Turn it off, Mom. And what are you doing out of bed?"

"Well, I heard you. What's that on your hand?"

"It's nothing. There was a broken window at the Brewers' and I had to board it up. I'll have to go back tomorrow and do it properly, but I cut myself on some glass."

"So let's put something on that. Come in the bathroom."

"Mom, just go back to bed."

"Not until we've put some iodine on that, and a bandage. Come along." She went into the bathroom and opened the first aid cabinet.

She washed his hand with warm water and soap and patted it dry. The cut was in the fleshy part at the base of his left thumb. Clean edges. She brushed on some iodine.

"Danny," she said, and she held his hand for the iodine to sink in. "I know it stings a bit, but it kills the germs. You didn't lend our boat to John Patrick so he could take those men out to Crieff, did you? Or take the kids, or anything like that? I have to ask, Danny."

"What? No, I didn't. What's all this suddenly?"

"You be honest with me, Danny."

"Mom. For heaven's sake. What's with you now? I had nothing to do with that. And neither did John Patrick."

"You don't know that. Letting him use our boat. You don't know what he did with it."

"But I do know. I know the man."

She peeled off gauze, then unspooled some tape and cut off two lengths.

"Nothing that big, Mom. It gets in the way. Just a good-sized Band-Aid."

"This needs more than a Band-Aid. Any deeper and it would need a couple of stitches." She cut the gauze and the tape smaller. "And you didn't take the men or the kids out yourself, did you?"

"No! Stop it now. I'm gett'n angry. I've never even seen those characters or the kids. I told you. And I told the policeman, and I told them at the morgue. I thought we were done with all that."

"Well, it turns out they were bringing in cocaine or something. The kids were. Probably. And those two men were meeting them. So how did they all get out to the island? Hold still now. I'm putt'n this on."

"How does anyone get out there? In a boat. Maybe they had their own."

"I hope that's all true, Danny. I want to believe you, that you had nothing to do with any of that."

"Well, I didn't. When did I ever lie to you?"

"I don't know. I hope never. Did you?"

"Never about anything important."

"I hope so." She pressed down the ends of the tape with her thumbs. "There," she said. "Don't get it wet."

"All right. Go to bed now, Mom. You're wearing me out." He took her by the shoulders and turned her around and out the bathroom door. "Night, Mom. Go to sleep."

Twenty-One

THE NEXT DAY Jack called to say they were sending him back to British Columbia. As he'd suspected. So even if he'd wanted to come out for that funeral, he couldn't.

Problems at the Tannhead silver mine, he said. And it was urgent. Metals were becoming a headache. Had she by any chance seen the price of silver? Twenty dollars an ounce and going up. And so of course they all wanted to increase production right away. He gave her the phone number of the mine office. A trailer camp in the bush, he said. He didn't know how long he'd be gone.

After she'd hung up she sat for a while looking at the telephone. It rang again, but it wasn't Jack. It was Hugh asking about progress with the new corporation transfer, the 65-million-dollar deal for a Hong Kong client. She told him she'd spoken with the client's office in London several times already and had begun writing a draft agreement. The case was progressing well, she said. She'd send him the draft in a day or two. The New York case was still in the research stage, and for the Hydro case she was planning a meeting in Toronto sometime in the week after Thanksgiving. Perhaps on that Thursday. Jenny was always fully informed, she said.

Aileen came with her to the hospital morgue, but then in the parking lot she changed her mind and said she'd rather wait in the car.

"Oh? Why?"

"Hospital politics. I'd just rather not be seen off-duty in there."

The pathologist was a woman her own age. Dr. Mary Snell, said her name tag. She led the way to a wall of steel drawers and put on glasses to search among the labels. She turned around to Margaret.

"Ready?"

Margaret nodded.

The drawers came out on rollers and rested side by side. The doctor drew back the sheets and there lay the children, pale and bare naked, with their eyes closed now and their hands one on top of the other on long, crudely stitched incisions down their chests and abdomens. Wide, clear faces. The girl had small breasts and fine-boned hands and nice fingernails. The boy had a small scar through the left eyebrow. Andrew had a little scar like that, in the other eyebrow, from some hockey practice on the Deer Park rink.

Behind her Dr. Snell stood and waited. After some time she cleared her throat and came forward.

"All right?" she said, and when Margaret nodded she pulled up the sheets and pushed the drawers shut again. She turned and led the way back up the concrete stairs and through the steel door into the lobby. There she stopped and turned around.

"You do know how they died?"

"Yes. More or less. Inspector Sorensen told me. She was probably standing right behind him."

"Yes, that's what it looks like. I understand you are hoping to arrange a funeral for them?"

"I am. In our church and our cemetery."

Dr. Snell nodded. "We'll have to wait for the paperwork. But good luck with it." She offered her hand.

After some minutes on the road, Aileen finally said, "So? Are you going to talk about it?"

And Margaret tried to describe what she had seen and how it had affected her. Talking about it helped, but it was still difficult. Both so very young and pale. Their dead, young faces up close. So utterly defenceless.

That afternoon she was at the co-op when Reverend McMurtry saw her and came up to her.

"Margaret," he said. "I should tell you, I am sorry but I have decided against it."

They were standing at the far end of the hardware section, where she'd found plastic tags and small nails to label her trees with. They were the only people there. He stood in his black suit and white collar, in his cracked black shoes. He was holding a brown paper bag with both hands.

"It's all just too irregular," he said. "Quite outside conventions. And I hear they may have been smugglers."

"They weren't *smugglers*. And even if. Does that matter? They were kids who made a mistake."

"Perhaps. But I wouldn't want their graves in our cemetery to become some sort of future romantic Bonnie and Clyde tourist attraction. Why not have them buried at La Roche, like your family?"

"I suppose I could, as a last resort, but they died here. Not on the North Shore."

"So did your grandmother, AJ."

"Oh, I see. It's because my grandmother wasn't buried here. Is that it?"

"No one from your family is buried here, Margaret."

"And you know why. Because there was a Joubert family plot in La Roche already and Grandmother wanted to be buried next to her husband."

"Well. Be that as it may. I have decided, and my answer is no." He took a step back and nodded at her, and turned and walked away.

"But they died here among us, Reverend," she said loudly to his back. "Doesn't that mean we have a certain obligation?"

He pretended not to hear, and she hurried after him. At the cash register they stood side by side. He paid and turned to go, stiff-necked and stubborn, and she told the clerk to weigh her nails and count the tabs and add it all up. She'd be back in a minute.

Outside he had just folded himself into his little Morris, and she walked up to it and put her hand on the door before he could close it.

"Reverend," she said. "Please wait! Did you hear what I said? What about our obligation as a community? Or even just an opportunity to come together as decent human beings. Have you thought about that?"

"Margaret, yes, I have thought about it. And I've given you my answer. Please let go of my door."

She did, and he slammed the door shut and started the engine and drove away.

Later she walked her forest to calm herself, and with the help of her father's book she began to identify trees from bark and needles and leaf arrangements. She printed each name with an indelible pen on a plastic tab and tacked that to the trunk.

Aileen saw her and came over. "Do you want some help with that?"

"You could hold this while I'm hammering. Thanks."

The nails were so small they were hard to hold with cold fingers and strike with the hammer. The second time she hammered her thumb and forefinger, Aileen said, "What's the matter? You're all fidgety."

And so she told her about the minister.

That evening and night she finished the draft agreement for Hong Kong, and in the morning to save time she took it directly to the courier office in Bridgewater. When she returned she was hardly out of the car when Aileen came hurrying, waving her arms.

"Margaret! Margaret! Wait! You won't believe what happened. The police took Danny's boat. It's over at Telford's yard."

"So get in the car. Quick. Where's Danny?"

"He's with them."

At the boatyard Telford and Sullivan and Danny stood in the open by the shed, and inside the shed the boat was up on a cradle and a man in a lab coat was working with a spray pump and a hand-held light that had a violet hue. A uniformed policeman stood guard at the ladder.

"In case you're wondering," Sully said to her, "the inspector has launched a new initiative to check on people with the right boats and the right skills, so Danny isn't the only one. I asked him if he agreed to a search of his boat, to eliminate it from a list of possibles, and he said yes."

"What right skills, Sergeant?"

"Finding their way in the dark, for one thing."

She looked over at Danny. "And you agreed. Is that right?"

"If it doesn't take too long. I don't mind. So they'll finally leave me alone."

She motioned for him to follow her to her car. She and Danny sat in the back and Aileen in the front.

"Danny, they are using a chemical called Luminol to search for blood. Blood is almost impossible to clean up completely, and under a special light even faint traces of it give off a bright glow. Are they going to find any blood in your boat?"

"I don't think so."

"You never rinsed out any blood?"

"No, I didn't. Well, for sure fish blood when I was still fishing."

"I am talking about human blood. They'll be able to tell the difference."

He shook his head.

"What about John Patrick? After he used your boat, did it ever look like it had been rinsed out?"

"It's a boat. It gets wet."

"Danny, this is serious."

"I know it is, and I have nothing to hide and I want to get it over with."

For a while she sat in silence. Aileen sat hunched in the passenger seat. She'd arranged the mirror so she could see them both in the back. Margaret could see her eyes and the worry in them.

She thought a while longer, then reached for the door handle.

"Wait," said Aileen. "I've been trying to keep quiet, but

what about the other night, Danny? When you had that cut on your hand. Show it to Margaret."

"Mom, that was nothing. I wish you'd stop butt'n in."

But he showed it to her and explained.

They walked back to the boat shed, and as soon as he saw them Sullivan came up and said that blood had been found in two places in the wheelhouse.

"Danny," she said. "Tell him."

And Danny showed the sergeant his hand and described the storm damage at the Brewers' property and how he'd cut himself taking out pieces of glass.

"All right," said Sullivan. "We'll check it out. And first thing tomorrow we'll need your blood sample. Have it done at the hospital and tell the nurse to call the police station for instructions. In the meantime we'll continue the search, and you can't use the boat. No one can. This is a suspect vessel now and it's got to stay put."

Sullivan turned to the constable. "I see there's a hasp on the door, so go over there and ask Mr. Herman if he has a padlock for it. If not, go and buy one. And when we're done, you stay here and you guard this situation. We'll spell you at the end of your shift."

—

At some point that night when she could not sleep, she went into Andrew's room again and turned on the ceiling light and sat in his driftwood chair. The silver Mother's Cross on the wall. His bucket full of lead.

She sat a while longer and tried to consider the possibility of turning the room into a guest room. Give away his clothes and the old chifforobe and the bed. Get modern furniture. A cheerful new rug. Pictures and new curtains. But it was unthinkable.

She turned out the light and went downstairs.

In the kitchen she made herself a cup of hot chocolate with real cocoa, milk, and sugar, something she had learned from Aileen, and then for a while she stood in the open back door. The trees darker than the night sky. By now she knew them from their outlines. White pine, red pine, tamarack, white spruce and the slimmer black spruce, a hemlock over there, a few cedars. And then the hardwoods, their leaves turning quickly now and beginning to fall.

Twenty-Two

ONE EVENING AT THÉRÈSE'S retirement residence in the South of France, five months after Andrew's death, there had been the outlines of trees against the sky as well, trees of a different kind. Palm trees, with pale light in the sky and pale light on the Mediterranean.

Over the years she and Thérèse had kept in touch and become friends, and that night they were sitting in canvas chairs on the patio, talking. Thérèse had a wool blanket over her knees even though it was May. She said she was often cold.

Thérèse was even thinner now, with a calm expression on her face nearly always. Her inner smile, as she'd once explained it to Margaret. Something she had taught herself. An inner smile through which to filter the world. What to allow in, what to keep out.

"Margaret," she said. "Do you remember the time when you sent me that note about holding rights and the Yes and No boxes?"

"Yes, of course I do."

"I thought so. At the time there was nothing more to be said about it, and it's many years ago, but I want to talk about it now. Because in the time since, I have changed my mind. Now, at this stage in my life—you understand, the person I am now, not the one I was then—I would mark the Yes box as well."

"You would? What happened?"

"Time happened. Now I would want to know. To be able to imagine him or her in later years. Mine would be fifty-four years old now. And it could be any woman or man out there. At the time I was in shock, Margaret. I despised that man, and I despised myself. I felt shamed. And I was so young. I knew nothing! The worst thing was that I blamed myself for the longest time."

"And yet you didn't keep it a secret."

"I did for the first little while. But once I had my teaching certificate and I heard about École Olivier and its philosophy, and that they were looking for someone to help build it, I made the decision, and from then on I even used it as a kind of qualification. A badge of merit. And it worked."

For a while they sat in silence. They could hear traffic from the street beyond the trees. A car door closing.

When Thérèse spoke again, she said that she had always liked Margaret's story about choosing parents at Lakewood. There was method and resolve in it. "Did it work?" she said.

"Mostly."

"And now?"

"On days when I'm not too shaky, it's still in a safe place."

Thérèse said she could understand that. Hers was in a safe place as well, and in some ways the entire episode had in the course of her life turned from a negative experience into a positive one, or at least an instructive one.

What she meant, she said, was that it had taught her to forgive herself and to be unafraid. And never again to allow herself to be shamed. It had made her into who she was, she said. And who with any luck she was still becoming. If she lived long enough.

Her hands were fingering the edge of the blanket. Dry hands. Thin, the veins dark.

"Other than that . . ." she said. "The saddest day of my life was when Philippe died. No, that's not true. The days that followed all the next year were even sadder. But you know that. We've talked about it. And still, to this day. So you see, Margaret? I do understand about loss."

There was silence between them for a while. Up in the palm trees, a breeze. Voices from somewhere.

"They'll be calling for dinner any moment now," Thérèse said. "The food's quite good here, you'll see. I'm so glad you came, Margaret. So very glad."

Thérèse had been at École Olivier for a total of nearly thirty years. She'd been there from the earliest stages and had helped build it into a fully academic finishing school, right up to the baccalaureate level.

But then, more than ten years after Margaret's time in France, two sets of parents made written complaints about Thérèse's unorthodox teaching. One of the complaints specifically mentioned her Women's Stories sessions. All too free and inappropriate, it said. Anti-Christian, anti-social, anti-family. At the very least, improper for girls that age.

An investigation followed. No real fault was found, and perhaps it was a coincidence that the girls whose parents had complained were friends and one of them had failed her baccalaureate. But the parents threatened to go directly to the Ministry of Education, and because the school's reputation mattered greatly in terms of its finances, Thérèse was asked to resign.

The dismissal was a blow to her, but it also set her free

to concentrate on her ideas around the inner self and fulfillment, and on her writing. She was fifty-five when she moved to furnished rooms and began helping in restaurant kitchens and serving at tables. She lived cheaply, like all the impoverished writers and poets in Paris, and set to work.

Her third and most famous book, *Between Me and Myself*, or *Entre moi et moi-même* in the original French, foreshadowed the bold new feminism to come and a woman's right, even obligation, to take full responsibility for herself and to make her own choices in all things related to her person. Reviewers called it absolutely scandalous, even shameless, and an affront to marriage and a woman's role within her family, but within less than a year *Between Me and Myself* was an international success.

In the dining room there were white tablecloths and flowers and good china and cutlery. Only subdued sounds came from the other tables in the room. Servers wore black skirts or trousers with long white aprons.

Over dinner she confided to Thérèse that in her darkest moments, when she leaned close to her bathroom mirror, she hated the person in there. And she feared that she'd become a good lawyer at a very high price. The law, she said, was after all only words. Lots of words that could be studied and remembered, and she was fortunate in that she was able at times to see connections that others had missed. But while success in her profession was one thing, she feared that she had failed at other things that normal women understood with perfect ease. Understood intuitively. Like how to keep your children close and safe, never mind how not to endanger your marriage.

Thérèse shook her head. "Give it time," she said. "And a *normal woman*—what is that? The best I can say is, give it time."

After dinner they walked to the taxi that would take her back to the hotel. Thérèse walked slowly, with her left arm in Margaret's. A more fragile arm now, and her hair nearly white, still perfectly groomed, still held up with combs. Black ones now.

At the bottom of the steps leading from the entrance to the street, Thérèse stopped. She reached and in the dark put her hand to Margaret's face and said, "About your sorrow, dear. There are no explanations, no reasons. And you know it. No one can take your sorrow away from you, or even lessen it for you. It is yours to bear, and after a while you will find that you can live with it. It will be a sweet pain close to your heart always, but in time that pain itself will become an important part of you. It is strange. It becomes almost something like a friend."

Twenty-Three

SHE STILL ALWAYS DRESSED in skirt, blouse, and jacket to work at her desk in the boathouse, and several times a day she dealt with couriers and spoke on the telephone with Jenny and at least once a day with Hugh Templeton. Hugh was pleased that the Chicago deal had gone through, and he'd signed off on the draft agreement for the Hong Kong corporation transfer.

On Wednesday from her desk she heard the sound of hammering and of workmen calling to one another. She picked up the pager and stepped into her boots and walked over to Aileen's to see what was going on.

"Cedar shingles," Aileen said with a big smile. "Can you believe it? Danny's early Christmas present to me. I had no idea he was planning on that. No idea at all. He's out in the truck right now since he doesn't have the boat."

Margaret called Inspector Sorensen to find out when the boat would be released, but the duty officer said the inspector was in Yarmouth on a case and might not be able to call back for a day or two.

Just before lunch she put on the coverall and walked over to Aileen's again, to help with the cleanup of the old shingles that had been stripped from the roof. They raked the broken pieces into piles on tarpaulins and the men dragged those across the rock to the truck and hoisted them up into the bed. For lunch Aileen served the workmen soft drinks and fish and chips and coleslaw at the picnic bench.

"Eat, boys. Eat," she kept urging them. For dessert, she brought a tub of ice cream and spoons and cups.

In Margaret's kitchen the light on the answering machine was blinking. It was Dr. Snell at the morgue, asking her to call back.

"Good news," said the doctor. "I have permission to release the bodies into your care. I'll need the name of the funeral home, and then you can come and sign some papers. Once the bodies are out of refrigeration they'll have to be cremated or buried within twenty-four hours. That's a public health requirement. Cremated, usually, because of the time constraint. When can you come?"

"Twenty-four hours. Wait, wait! I didn't know that. I'll have to make arrangements. Don't take them out just yet. Let me call you back."

She showered and then put on city clothes and a coat and drove to the church.

This time the minister did not even ask her to sit.

He stood listening to her, and when she had finished he shook his head. "I haven't changed my mind, Margaret. I think about these things carefully and then I decide. I have decided. I'm sorry, but the answer is still no."

"But why, Reverend?"

"I've told you why."

"But have you considered how good it would be for the community to come together for this cause? Have you spoken to people, had anyone's input? Or is it just your own opinion, your possibly quite stubborn opinion, if I may say so?"

He opened his mouth to say something, but she went on. "Bonnie and Clyde graves indeed. And what if? Would that be so bad? Reverend, I am asking you to reconsider. A church service. No coffins and open graves, just two urns, as it turns out. And let's say a small memorial plaque on the urn wall, which I'll pay for."

She tried to calm herself, to smile at him.

"Please, Reverend. May I remind you of how much my family, especially my grandmother, has done for this community and this church? The town hall in her name, AJ Hall, and the fund she set up for its maintenance."

"The grandmother who is not laid to rest here among us. Nor is her husband, nor your father. And neither, I imagine, will you be."

"Reverend, please think about it a bit more."

She waited for him to say something but he just shook his head. He raised a hand and waved at his desk. "I have work to do, Mrs. Bradley. But thank you for your visit."

On the way home she made a detour past the boatyard. Down at the shed the same constable was back, guarding the door. He sat with his collar up and his hands in his armpits for warmth, on a kitchen chair with a brick under each front leg to make it even. When he saw her he stood up.

"Ma'am," he said.

"Constable. Any news in the case? About Danny's blood test? Do you know?"

"No, ma'am. You'd have to speak with the inspector about that. And ma'am, what if a storm hits while I'm out here? Do you think I could move inside somewhere? Maybe that shed down there. Would that be all right?"

"Seems reasonable to me, Constable. But you better check with the sergeant."

From the house she called Sorensen again and left

another message. She called the station and asked for Sergeant Sullivan and was told by the desk officer that the sergeant was out as well.

Up in Andrew's room she opened the window wide. She propped the door open and walked across the landing into the other room and opened that window and then kept the door open also. She stood in the draft, feeling it.

In his closet she reached and pushed his clothes to the far right on the rod. There weren't many of them. Two pairs of dress pants, jeans, a sports jacket, and some shirts. The brick-red linen one that he'd liked best. His jean jacket. The drawers were nearly empty as well. A shirt she didn't recognize. Some socks. She stripped his bed and stood up the two mattress segments and leaned them against each other. She picked up the sheets and pillow-cases and carried them down to the washing machine. The solenoid clicked and warm water rushed in, and when the soap powder was dissolved she put in the sheets and closed the lid.

Throughout all this she kept talking to him. Hoping he would not mind, would understand. It was only when she was back at the kitchen table that she realized she was crying. At the sink she threw water on her face and dabbed it dry with a paper towel and sat down again at the table with her hands in her lap.

Not long thereafter Sullivan's car turned into her driveway. He said he'd come to tell her that the report on Danny's blood was in, and it was inconclusive. His blood type was O positive, which was the same as some of the blood on the dock and in his boat. It was a common blood group, and so his sample and the scrapings from the boat would have to be sent to a special lab for a more detailed analysis.

"I see. But while he waits, can he have his boat back? He needs it for his work. This is the storm season, and he's behind already."

"Well. No. He can't get it back until this is all done. Until the results are back from Ottawa."

"And how much longer will that take?"

"I really don't know."

When the sergeant had left, she changed out of her dress into jeans and a sweater. She put on her coat and then reached for her purse and keys and drove into town. At the Save-Easy she bought the newspaper and milk, and down the coast at the Outrigger restaurant she bought takeout food.

There had been a time when she had enjoyed cooking.

Her main inspiration early on had been the sauce chef at Le Boeuf d'Or. He had liked her, and one Saturday after lunch he'd shown her his station and his implements, and in tones as solemn as a priest's he had talked about sauces and drippings and cognac and port wine and dried fruit chopped very fine, and long, long simmering and reducing, and at a near whisper he talked about his herbs, never chopped fine but left long in their stalks so they could be removed, some indeed to be removed after only minutes, others after half an hour. And she'd understood and enjoyed all that. Found it interesting, not only because it echoed Manssourian's notion about dancing with life, but also because in French cuisine the sauce was often the one distinctive taste that lingered.

Now at her kitchen table she flipped through the business section of the newspaper and noted the prices of silver, copper, and nickel. Silver was twenty-two dollars an ounce now, up two dollars since Jack's last call. How much had it been a few months ago? She had no idea what any of the commodity prices meant in terms of market swings. Fluoride, there. How much was that? She knew he had developed at least two fluoride mines, one in Italy, the other in Bavaria.

She found a piece of paper and a pencil and wrote down some questions to ask him about his work the next time he called. She might stay in this chair and read the business section now. There was often a mining segment. She looked over at the telephone on the wall. Call me, she said to him.

Silver. She'd been three months pregnant with Andrew when she went with Jack on a trip to Turkey, into the heart of Anatolia. He'd been sent there by a mining company to report on a silver property they were considering bidding on.

They flew over the land in a small airplane and she sat behind him, nervous about him leaning so far out the window. At one point she held him back by his belt. He brought his head in and grinned at her, and then he asked the pilot to fly as low as possible so he could make exact notes for landmarks on his geo-map. Next day they had a guide and they travelled on horseback. Three saddle horses and two packhorses with tents and food.

It was her first experience of Jack at work. He'd walk the land and stop and go down and chip at rocks with his hammer. He'd examine pieces with his twelve-times magnifier. In a rise he found what he called a flowstone bubble, and he put on a hard hat and crawled into the cave and down so far she could no longer see his flashlight

or hear his hammer. After a while he came back. He was
dragging something heavy.

What is it? she said.

Hold out both hands and see.

He put it in her hands, and it was a chunk of rock half
enclosing a lump of pure native silver the size of a man's fist.

That's a few hundred million years old, he said. It could
be from an impact that melted things when the universe
was still crowded with circling lumps crashing into each
other. Or when some of this was still hot and bubbling.

At ten-thirty that night he did call. Six-thirty his time, he
said.

"Were you already in bed?"

"No. Not yet."

She told him about Danny's blood test, the locked-up
boat, and the new roof. And that the children had been
released into her care, but now the minister was refusing
to hold a service for them.

"But I haven't given up yet," she said. "And I aired out
Andrew's room and stood up the mattresses and washed
the sheets."

It was a simple housekeeping task, but because of the
stark image of the mattress segments leaning against each

other in the empty bed it sounded enormous to her, even just mentioning it.

Jack must have sensed that because he said nothing for a while.

"Did you," he said then.

"We could get different furniture for that room."

"We could. If you want to."

"When are you coming back?"

"I don't know yet. And you?"

"I was thinking after Thanksgiving, if Hugh lets me. I can work fine here, and this place is helping me. I think I'm getting better, Jack. Maybe about everything. Even the headaches."

She reached for her notes on the kitchen table.

"I see that silver is up again," she said.

"Yes, it is."

"I was remembering our trip to Anatolia, Jack. The company did lease that property, didn't they?"

"They did, and it was a good producer for a long time before the cost-benefit ratio dipped. There are new extraction methods now, but they are controversial."

"Jack," she said. "If the funeral for the kids is in a week or so, are you sure you wouldn't want to come out?"

There was a pause and then he said, "Margaret, please don't ask me that again. No, I wouldn't, and I couldn't. We've just moved new machinery to the face, and there's no way I'd take time off to fly four time zones across the country for the funeral of two kids I don't even know."

"You'd be doing it for me. Not for the kids."

"I know that. Let it go. Please."

After a while he said, "How are you really doing, Maggie?"

When she didn't reply he told her he was calling from the mine office, which was the only place with a phone. His voice had softened. He described to her what the camp was like and what he saw looking out the window. Three-thousand-foot mountains, snowy peaks, and snow-fields orange in the setting sun. Tall evergreens nearby, and at the edge of the camp one tree so big that three men could not hold hands around it.

She sat back in the chair and listened to the tone of his voice, while all beyond the kitchen the house was dark and quiet.

Twenty-Four

REVEREND MCMURTRY CAME OUT to bless the new roof, and all of Aileen's friends and neighbours were invited to the celebration. It was a ceremony that had been customary in the early days along this coast, and the minister had recently brought it back. After the roof blessing he stayed for a while to mingle. Aileen served food and drink, and Pete Woolner, who had once been a fisherman but now drove the school bus, played the accordion, and someone had brought a tin whistle and someone else a washboard and spoons. People's cars and pickups were parked on the gravel road and on Margaret's property.

Throughout the event the minister avoided her, but as he left she followed him to his car.

"Reverend," she said. "Please wait. Isn't there perhaps

something I can say or do to make you reconsider about the funeral service?"

"Oh dear. Please not that again, Mrs. Bradley."

He opened the door to his Morris and squeezed in and quickly shut the door. But he did crank down the window. She put her hand on the frame and he looked at it wearily.

"Reverend, please," she said. "Wouldn't it be good for this dying community?"

"Is it dying?"

"Well, of course it is. What are its prospects? Where are the young people? The fishing's just about killed off, and even the tire factory is running half shifts now. Look at the numbers, Reverend. And look at the turnout for this roof blessing. How we appreciate every opportunity to congregate and shake hands! A funeral service for two strange young people who've died here among us, far from their parents. The dignity accorded them. Imagine the turnout, Reverend. The good feeling for your church."

He started his engine and shifted into reverse. Then he shifted back into neutral and let out the clutch and turned to her.

"Margaret, you speak plainly, so let me do the same. I knew your grandmother all my young life. She died when I was away at the seminary. AJ was one of the most generous and independent, but also one of the most maddeningly stubborn people I ever came across, to put it mildly. But she knew what she wanted, and I admired that. And then your father and his forest conservation project. For how many years did he work on it? *Years*, Margaret. *Years*. And now we have you and your relentless crusade for these dead, unknown young people."

He shook his head. But there was the hint of a smile on his face now.

He looked away from her, down past his knees for the right pedal, and he shifted and backed up and shifted again. He turned to her and nodded goodbye, and then he cranked his wheel furiously and drove away. A moment later his hand came out the little window and waved to her.

Later that day a hard wind came up and it began to rain again. The wind came from a long fetch across open water, and at times it blew so hard and steady that the rain came nearly sideways past her kitchen window. She was waiting for Inspector Sorensen. He had called because the results of Danny's blood test were in, and he'd said he wanted to talk to her about that and about something else.

When he arrived he parked on her rock and then hurried toward the house clutching his hat with both hands. She held the door open for him.

"Wild," he said. "Did it ever stop since last time?"

"It did. This just started a little while ago and it'll calm down again. But this is our storm season, and it'll get much worse. At some point we tie our houses down. Literally. We have steel trusses for that, on this stretch of the coast, with our onshore winds."

He hung up his coat and hat, and they sat again at the kitchen table.

"So," he said. "You'll be glad to hear that the blood in the wheelhouse of Danny's boat is his all right, and his story about the broken window checks out."

"Does that mean he can have his boat back?"

"Yes, it does. Sergeant Sullivan will give him a signed release. But there's something else I wanted to tell you. We've made some progress in our search for people with the right boats and the right skills, and now we're pretty sure we know who did the Crieff Island run that night. We haven't found the man himself yet, but we found his truck and it had blood in the passenger seat. The blood of the man who got slashed on the dock and lost his shoe."

"Who's the owner of the truck?"

"I can't tell you that. But we have a warrant out for him."

"You can't tell me who he is?"

"I can't release the name yet, but I can tell you that he's an old fisherman. A former fisherman."

"We have many of those. Maybe they stole his truck."

"It's possible. We'll find that out when we talk to him. We went to his place but there was no one there. The neighbours haven't seen him in a while. We asked at the marina and he hasn't been seen there in a while either."

"And his boat?"

"We're looking for it."

"So what happens next?"

"Detail work. We'll keep looking. After a while we'll post a public warrant for him and the boat."

For a moment they sat in silence. They could hear the wind and the rain. The house creaked in its joinery, and Sorensen cocked his head and turned and looked around the room.

"That's just the wind," she said. "The roof structure is tied directly into the full frame, and it's all pegged with what they called trunnels or treenails. In a strong blow the house actually changes shape. Fractionally. Like a ship at sea."

He shook his head. "It's all so different down here. And the people too. So scrappy. Like your Aileen. The first time I met her she just about bit my head off. In the meantime, I've come to like little Sweetbarry. Why is it spelled that way, with an *a*?"

"We don't know. It's written that way in the founding scroll at the town hall. Maybe it's the scribe's fault. But

I'm sorry, I haven't offered you any coffee yet. Would you like some? Or some cornbread and olives?"

He shook his head. "No time. But thank you."

After he'd left she waited a while, and when the weather had calmed somewhat she stepped into her boots and put on her father's old slicker and cap and walked next door. She found Danny pacing the rock, searching the ground for nails.

"Danny," she shouted. "Good news. You can have your boat back. But there's something else that's not so good."

When she got back to the house there was a message on the machine, and she rewound the tape and listened. It was the minister saying that he wasn't sure what it was, but something about their last conversation was making him willing to reconsider about the funeral service. He said it wasn't so much her Joubert stubbornness but more what she'd said about the community. And he cared about the community. It was the reason why he'd brought back the roof blessing. In addition to that, he said, he'd been reminded that sinners before man-made laws may not be sinners before God.

"So yes, Margaret. I make no promises, but come and talk to me. Tell me again what you have in mind."

She was smiling. She played the tape a second time, then she put on her good coat and shoes and pocketed the pager, and drove to the church.

THE PARENTS

Twenty-Five

ON THE DAY OF THE CREMATION she and Aileen and Franklin and the funeral director were the only people present.

There had been a conversation at the undertaker's about how the children should be clothed. The choice was hers, the funeral director had said. He recommended the usual white shifts. Most corpses were clothed that way. Good Indian cotton cloth, cut loosely and buttoned at the back like hospital gowns.

"Really? My grandmother was fully dressed, and so was my father."

"Not for cremation. I took the liberty to look up the history and both were full burials, and they were dressed for a viewing."

"Yes. You're right."

He waited a moment, then said, "So. White gowns?"

She agreed, and he wrote that down.

"And on their feet?" she said.

He looked up from his clipboard. "Barefoot is customary, Mrs. Bradley. What did you have in mind?"

"I don't know. But barefoot?"

"Well, I suppose . . . I suppose we could do white socks. Would that be all right?"

And she nodded.

"White socks, then, Mrs. Bradley. I'll make a note of that."

Later in the sample room she'd chosen medium trim with acanthus leaves and bevelled edges on a black plywood coffin, and she'd bought black picture frames and in them mounted the drawings of the children as they had looked in life.

Now the first coffin lay ready on the conveyor belt, and she and Aileen and Franklin sat in the front pew in the small chapel at the crematorium. On the coffins lay the flowers that she'd bought at the Save-Easy that morning. The conveyor belt ended at a purple velvet curtain, and the pictures of the children stood next to a vase with more flowers on a small table to one side of that curtain. The second coffin lay ready on trestles against a wall.

That day at the office the funeral director had said it was not often that they fired two coffins at once. Complete incineration took a while, and they might wish to be present only for the symbolic moments of the first one. Until they saw the flames, he said, and then the gate and curtain would be closed again and the burners turned up to full power.

Now in his black suit and grey vest and grey gloves he stood ready at a panel of buttons. He asked if anyone wished to say a few words, and Aileen looked at her. She shook her head, but then she stood up and walked up to the coffins one by one and placed a bare hand on them and stood for a moment.

When she was back in her pew the funeral director turned to the panel and pushed the first button. The lights dimmed and the purple curtain moved aside and the furnace door opened. The coffin began to move forward, and inside the furnace a moving steel grid took over. When the coffin had come to rest, blue gas flames could be seen, and then the flames grew. In the heat the paint blistered and curled, and moments later the wood itself caught fire and soon all they could see were flames.

The furnace door slid shut and the curtain before it, and a great roaring sound came from within. They listened to the flames for a while, and when the house lights came back up they rose and stepped out of the pew. At the chapel entrance the funeral director had taken off his gloves and he shook their hands.

—

They drove home to Sweetbarry in silence. The clouds to nor'east had piled up again, heavy and black. Purple at the base, as if squeezed and condensed under the pressure of all the weight above. Gusts of wind and spits of rain against the windshield.

She could see Franklin in the rear-view mirror, in an old wool suit, from when he was a much younger man, and a white shirt and black tie. Clean-shaven and with a fresh haircut that showed white skin on his neck. He nodded at her in the mirror.

They drove on. A misty, grey day. Silver days, her father used to call them. Along the way, tall reeds in the bracken ponds lay beaten flat, and rags of foam lifted off the water and sailed across the road.

An hour later she and Franklin sat in Aileen's kitchen, and Aileen had made coffee for them. The window was open a crack because the entire house smelled strongly of the fermenting blueberry wine.

"How's the new batch coming?" said Margaret. "It's rich enough in here to get high on just the fumes."

"I know. I keep them covered like babes and I'm

airing the place out as often as I can. It'll be up to twelve or thirteen per cent now. Usually it finishes around sixteen. The flavour is great then but it's pretty dry, and so when it stops working it's siphoned off and we add a bit of sugar. In the bottle it keeps getting better all the time."

Out the window against the dark of rocks and evergreens, small snowflakes were drifting by.

"You see that?" said Franklin. "So early. Is Danny out on his rounds?"

"He is. I did tell him to keep his head down and not to take any chances with the boat. To stay away from John Patrick."

Just then a police car pulled up, and Sullivan climbed out and put on his uniform cap.

"Oh-oh," said Aileen. "I don't like seeing that boy show up like that."

He came up the stoop and walked past the kitchen window. The door opened and then from the little hallway he called, "Hello? Mrs. McInnis?"

"In the kitchen, Sergeant."

He came in with his cap off, and he looked at them in their chairs with their mugs on the table. He raised his nose to the alcohol fumes but said nothing.

"Take a seat, Sergeant," said Aileen. "Want some coffee?"

He shook his head and remained standing. He looked away from Aileen, over at Margaret.

"Mrs. Bradley, I have an urgent message for you. I went to your house first but there was no one there. Inspector Sorensen wants you to know that the parents of the dead kids have come forward. The inspector wants you to stop everything you're doing in connection with the case. Every last thing, ma'am. Right away. And he's asking you to be ready to take his phone call at noon today at your number."

She stood in her bathroom and opened the medicine cabinet and took out the pills. She uncapped the bottles and slid out one of the antianxiety pills and one of the new stronger codeines. She held them ready in her fingers but then put them down on the glass shelf.

He called at exactly twelve o'clock.

"I heard," she said. "You found the parents. Of both of them?"

"There's only one set of parents. The kids were brother and sister."

"Brother and sister."

"Yes. That's one test we didn't do. The truth is, I didn't think of it. Anyway, they are here now. Somebody, I think a teacher, saw the posted pictures at a police station in

Mexico and recognized them. The parents speak English quite well. I understand you've had the bodies picked up. Where are they now, so the parents can go and view them?"

"But it's too late for that! They've been cremated."

There was silence on the line.

"Already," he said then. "That's very unfortunate. They wanted to take them home."

She felt dizzy for a moment. "Well, I . . . there were public health regulations. Once they were out of refrigeration. The funeral is on Tuesday."

"Maybe not. You may need to cancel it. Can you come into the city and talk to the parents? Tell them how it happened. Your part in it. Explain about the funeral. Do you have the ashes?"

She heard what he was saying but she was far away, pressing her fingers to her eyebrow.

"Mrs. Bradley?"

"Can I call you back on this? I'll call you back . . ."

She put the receiver down on the table and walked into the bathroom and put both pills in her mouth. Bit on them and moved the crumbs under her tongue and then walked into the living room and sat down on the sofa, leaning forward with her eyes closed and her face in her cupped hands.

At some point she could hear sounds in the kitchen, and when she turned there was Aileen walking her way with a folded damp cloth.

"I called but there was always just the busy signal," said Aileen. "So I came over. Lean back and let's put this on your forehead. Let me help you, Margaret."

Three hours later she felt better. She was in her car, driving into the city. Rather than the highway, she took the old coastal route through the small towns. Chester, East River, and the peninsular route from there, the ocean always to her right, through Blandford and Bayswater and Fox Point and Black Point and Upper Tantallon, and on to the city.

She checked into the Westin and sat for a while on the side of the bed with her hands in her lap. It was six-thirty on Saturday evening. Out the window it was getting dark. She could see the reflection of the room, the bed and the lamp on the side table. Herself sitting there, all in black except for the grey blouse. Lights coming on everywhere, pinpoints of light.

When she'd made the decision, she took the elevator two floors up and walked along the hallway. In front of their door she raised her hand and knocked.

Voices from inside, then the door was opened by a man in a black suit and tie. She said her name and the man nodded and motioned her into the room. She could see a woman lying on the bed, propped up by a pillow against the headboard. She wore a long black dress, and as Margaret stepped into the room the woman drew a black veil down over her head and face. On a small white plate on the side table next to the only chair in the room, a candle was burning.

She had brought the framed drawings of the children, and she placed them on the bed and reached to touch the woman's hand but the woman moved her hand away.

The man said something softly to her in Spanish but the woman ignored him.

They stood awkwardly for a moment, and then the man offered his hand and shook hers and pointed at the chair.

He said, "My wife, Anna, the children's mother, she is in very mourning. We both are." He looked at the woman and again said a few words in Spanish.

"She is in very mourning," he said again to Margaret. "She requests to be excused because a large part of her is not here in this room."

He studied the small black bowtie in Margaret's lapel and said something else to the woman. She whispered some words and held out her hand for the pictures, and the man passed them to her. He sat down on the side of the bed with his hands on his black trouser knees. They were strong, well-shaped hands, good hands, much like Jack's.

The woman looked at the pictures through her veil for a long time while no one spoke. Then she put them down by her side. For a while they could hear her weeping. She sat with her glasses in one hand and with the other using a tissue behind the veil.

"Their names were Hugo and Carmensita," said the man. "They were young, with so much still to learn about this world. Which is a treacherous world, unforgiving of mistakes and weakness. Even in the case of so much innocence."

"Yes, it is," said Margaret. "I don't know where to begin. The inspector has told you, yes? About the cremation and the planned funeral service?"

The woman spoke some words in Spanish to the man, and he nodded slowly and looked at Margaret.

He said, "Anna wants to know why you are wearing a brazal de luto."

"Mourning ribbon," said the woman, and he repeated those words.

Margaret put her hand to her lapel and said, "It is for my son. He died in January of this year. He was in training to become a military pilot."

"A soldier," said the woman. "In which war?"

"He died in a peacekeeping mission."

"A peacekeeping mission."

"Yes."

The man and the woman sat waiting for her to go on, but she did not. After a while the man stood up from the bed and went into the bathroom. He came back with a glass of water, and he raised it and wiped the bottom with his hand and then set it carefully on the low table next to Margaret's chair.

He returned to the side of the bed and sat again with his hands on his knees. The woman now reached and folded up her veil. She had a strong, pale face and black hair pulled back and twisted forward over one shoulder.

"Please tell us about our children," she said. "The inspector said only what was in the police report. And that they found us too late, and that you were planning a funeral. Please tell us more. For example, why the cremación."

When she had described and explained as best she could, there was a lengthy silence. The woman had drawn the veil back down over her face, and again she held her glasses in one hand and with the other used a tissue.

Margaret stood up and approached the woman on the bed and offered her hand again. The woman lifted the veil and put on her glasses and took Margaret's hand. Then she leaned her head back against the pillow and closed her eyes. She reached blindly for the veil and lowered it again over her face. She spoke some words in Spanish to her husband and he nodded and stood up.

"With your permission, Anna is asking for you please to excuse us now," he said. "She is very sad today. I am also."

Twenty-Six

IN THE MORNING she called them on the telephone and offered to take them to St. Mary's Cathedral for mass. They agreed, and half an hour later they met in the hotel lobby. They shook hands, and the woman said formally that her name was Anna and her husband's was Gustavo.

Margaret said her name as well, and she told them that her husband Jack could not be here because he had to travel a great deal. He was a mining geologist.

The man said, "Geólogo?" to the woman, and she nodded. To Margaret she said, "Gustavo and I are teachers. Carmensita was going to be as well. Hugo had not decided."

They were again clothed all in black, Anna in her long dress and a hat with a black veil. People in the hotel lobby stole glances at them.

The church was one of the oldest on the coast. It had high vaults of stone and wood joinery and tall leaded windows, and all the woodwork and the very stone were steeped in incense for generations.

At communion the parents went up to the rail and knelt. When the priest offered the mother the host, she raised her veil and he placed it on her tongue and she lowered the veil again and bowed her head. The father had the host put into his cupped hands.

After the service she took them back to the hotel, and from her room she called the minister and explained. No ceremony at the urn wall, she said, because the parents would be taking the ashes home with them. Just the memorial service.

The parents had not wanted breakfast and they would not eat lunch. But they sat with her at the table and spoke mostly English with each other for her benefit. They sipped water and told her about their children. They were much the same stories she might have told about Andrew. Sweet and adorable when they were small, more and more strong-willed and independent as they grew older. A fine closeness between brother and sister. Acts of rebellion from the boy. He ran away from home once when he was sixteen, but in the night threw pebbles at his sister's window and let her know where he was. And in the morning she went there and persuaded him to come home.

"And where was he?" Margaret asked.

"In the small Santa María Chapel. Our bigger churches are locked at night now."

"In a chapel. Was he religious?"

"Not really. But it was raining. And he'd been an altar boy in primary school. I sewed his sobrepelliz." The mother ran her hands over her front. "All white, and a small cross here," she said.

She reached up and let the veil fall over her face. She opened her purse and took out a handkerchief and snapped shut the purse and sat back in her chair.

In the afternoon they drove south to Sweetbarry. The parents were in the back seat. She took the coastal road again, the ocean always to their left, the small, solitary white houses like stranded lifeboats. She felt proud of it all, loved to hear them comment to each other and in her limited Spanish knew enough words to follow their exchanges.

Halfway there, the mother said, "Tell us about your son, please."

And she found it a welcome relief to tell them all that was on her mind while they sat in the back seat, listening.

She told them about Andrew's schooling to become an engineer, and about his dream to become a military pilot; about the last time she saw him, hoisting his duffel bag, so eager to get on that bus. The grinning faces in the windows, boys going off on their big adventure. She saw that last happy moment so often, she said. And she would tell herself, Remember that. Remember that. So very often. As if she could still not believe it. As if by recalling it, she might be able to make it real again and then undo it. Change the outcome.

They drove on. At some point the father cleared his throat and then spoke for the first time, unprompted and at length. He spoke with great formality.

"Señora Bradley," he said. "With your permission. Anna and I always said that we must allow our children to make their own mistakes, small mistakes, and learn from them. Some of their own decisions. We never imagined that any outcome could be so unforgiving. You speak of your son leaving you that day on the bus, but perhaps it was not *you* he was leaving. Perhaps men, young and old, embark on adventures to discover themselves, as the storybooks tell. And to pry themselves loose from the familiar, the safe. The predictable.

"We cannot change our children's nature, we can only hope to guide them somewhat. Anna and I, we talk about this, and we very much want to think that this is true. That they set out on the necessary journey, a journey of which they cannot know the ending, but at the time of setting out, the ending is not important. It is the journey that matters. And endings such as that of your son and our children, how can they be foreseen? They cannot. They are unknowable."

Anna said something to him in Spanish, and he replied gently in English that it was true and that it was important.

"Señora Bradley," he said, "our son loved his sister, but this adventure was surely his idea. The newspapers are writing of other students doing it. It is new but already quite common. An act of independence and a thrill, and as much as four thousand American dollars in cash per carrier. In many places in our country you can buy a house for that. And it is all prepared and organized like a guided tour, and always they come back safe. Until now. But you see the temptation for the young? The attraction?

"We cannot know what happened on that island. Perhaps he fought a man and tried to protect his sister. And she had come along perhaps to protect him. You see? We cannot know. The only thing that is certain is that their mother and I will always love them and we will be sad for a long time, perhaps always."

They drove on in silence. Through Marriott's Cove, through Western Shore. When she could see the steeple of St. Peter's in the distance she slowed the car and pointed it out to them. That was where the service would be held on Tuesday, she said.

In the rear-view mirror she could see them sitting close together. Anna was not wearing the veil now. She had her glasses off and was dabbing at her eyes with a tissue.

They sat with their heads and shoulders so close together that not one sliver of daylight could be seen between them.

At the house she put them up in Andrew's room. She levelled the mattresses and put fresh linens on the bed. She carried away the lead bucket and the driftwood chair and brought in chairs from the other bedrooms. Then she let them rest for a while.

She put a note for them on the kitchen table and then drove down to the Outrigger. The restaurant was busy. Warm and cosy inside, with burning candles on the tables. Windows overlooking the wooden dock with yellow light bulbs on wires and two deep-sea fishing boats tied to wooden bollards. She stood inside the door and motioned to Tammy.

"What's up, Margaret?" Tammy said. "This morning

the minister told us about the service for the dead kids on Tuesday. Brother and sister they were, he said. Oh my God. That's so sad!"

"Isn't it."

"We'll surely all be there on Tuesday."

"Good. Listen, I've got the parents staying with me. They haven't eaten all day and I want to serve them a nice dinner. What's on tonight?"

"Ah. The special is fresh-caught haddock. The *Mary-Beth* came in just a few hours ago. You can serve it with yellow beans and parsley potatoes from the valley. Maybe take those cooked and heat them and take the fish raw. Do the fillets pan-fried in butter. A bit of salt and pepper on it. They'll love it, Margaret. Don't overcook the fish. No more than a minute or so on each side."

The next day the parents went for a long walk in borrowed slickers over their black clothes, down the shore path to the lighthouse and the sentinel rocks, and back through town.

They rested in their room, and then Margaret served them tea and sat with them for a time. For dinner she cooked a ham, and Aileen made the side dishes. With Aileen, Franklin, and Danny present they were six around the table. They sat with their heads bowed while the father said grace in Spanish.

"Bendícenos, Señor, bendice estos alimentos que por tu bondad vamos a recibir . . ."

During the meal he asked about Jack, and she said that Jack was a few thousand miles away, at a silver mine on the other side of the country. The father said he taught geography and the earth's history and Anna taught English and Spanish literature. Aileen tried to engage Anna in conversation but Anna hardly spoke at all. Before long she excused herself and never came back to the table. The father went to look after her, and when he came back downstairs he too asked to be excused.

"With your permission," he said. "Anna, my wife, is very sad. And she is tired. I will be with her now. Thank you for everything. You are very kind."

He inclined his head to the group around the table.

Next morning on the way to church there was dense fog, and wet leaves covered the ground. She drove with the flashers going and the low beams on.

At the church Franklin in his wool suit served as a greeter, and he shook their hands and the hands of the parents and showed them to the front pew, where Aileen and Danny were already seated. People leaned forward to see the parents, and then the first few began to file out of their pews and line up before the father and the mother in her veil. They bowed their heads and murmured condolences, and before long the entire centre aisle was filled with people waiting to do the same.

The urns stood on the Lord's Table, which was a long slab of stone on rough-hewn trestles, covered with a white cloth. A small upright wooden crucifix and six lit candles were the only other objects on the table. The urns were burnished metal containers with screw tops.

When the people had stopped coming forward, the mother raised her veil and walked up to the urns. The father followed, but then he stood back. She put her hands on the urns and then picked them up one at a time and held them to her cheeks. She stood with each urn for a long moment and then set it back on the table.

When the parents had returned to their pew, Reverend McMurtry climbed the steps to the pulpit. He held up his hands and let them fall. He said that the congregation had come together that day to say farewell to Hugo and Carmensita, two young people who had died here among them. And that they were gathered here also to give support and warmth as a community to the bereaved parents.

He spoke about God's open arms and about the end of life on earth also being a new beginning, and when he had stepped down from the pulpit, old Mr. Thompson, who normally on a weekday would be pumping gas at the co-op, walked up to the Bible stand and found his page and began to read.

"Teach us to number our days," he read, "that we may gain a heart of wisdom . . ."

At one point the main door must have been opened and kept open for a while, because in the church they could suddenly smell the ocean and the cold salt air, and on the Lord's Table the candle flames twisted and smoked and then stood straight again.

Up in the loft Miss Belvedere began to play the mother's lament that Margaret had asked her to play, from Gustav Mahler's *Songs upon the Death of Children*. And with the second line of music, Joan Hendricks by her side began to sing.

The parents spent the rest of the day in their room. Margaret brought them lunch and then tea and candles and matches. She brought in a third chair and sat with them in the late afternoon gloom by the light of a single candle.

For a while they talked about their children, but soon they fell silent. She tried to think of more things to say that might help them and help her, but there was nothing. Nothing beyond the good words the father had spoken during the car ride down about human journeys and allowing children to make their own mistakes, and two days later even those words seemed to miss the point.

Behind their thoughts, if they could slow them enough, they could feel this moment passing into this, and then this and this. They could hear the water and the rocks. They could hear seabirds and the wind in the trees, and in the last grey light of day they could hear the fox. Four, five sharp barks close by, and the last one the rising note, like no other sound anywhere. When they heard it, the parents raised their heads and looked at each other and then at her, and Margaret explained about the mother fox and her cubs, and that they were denning not far away.

The father looked confused.

"Es un zorro," Anna explained to him. "En realidad una zorra, con dos cachorros. Viven aquí."

"Una zorra," he said. His face relaxed, then he nodded and looked over at Margaret and smiled.

Not long thereafter she asked them down to dinner. Aileen had brought over a tureen with a lobster dish and left it on the kitchen table with a note to them. Margaret made a little green salad and opened a bottle of white wine, and then they sat down, the three of them around one corner of the table. Out the window it was night now. There was some silver still in the sky to the west, and the trees were darker than the sky. A half moon behind the white pine by her driveway.

In the morning it was raining and blowing hard. They were about to climb into the car for the drive to the airport when Anna paused and straightened and turned to Margaret. For a moment they stood with their hands on their hats and the wind tearing at their clothes.

"I saw the cruz de plata, of course," said Anna. "The mother's medal they gave you. And yesterday I suddenly understood completely why this funeral, and why the cremación. I do not know why not sooner. I do not know."

She let go of her hat with one hand and gave Margaret a one-armed embrace. "We will be friends," she said. "You will see."

THE WAY HOME

Twenty-Seven

AT THE AIRPORT she stood at a payphone, and with two stacks of dimes and quarters in front of her dialled the number of the trailer camp in British Columbia. Someone picked up and she asked for Jack Bradley, and moments later there was his voice.

"Can you talk for a minute, Jack?"

"Yes. Of course."

She told him about the parents. That they had just left and she missed them both already. Their closeness, she said. The way they stood together as one. It had helped her in ways she had yet to understand completely. She described the funeral service, the people lining up in the aisle to meet them.

She kept feeding coins into the machine and went on to describe how she'd sat with them up in Andrew's room. How after a while the silence had become peace.

She said, "I'd like to stay here until Thanksgiving. I haven't told Hugh yet, but I think he'll let me. Do you think you could come out for that? Can I ask you that? Please? I don't know your work situation right now, but could we have a few quiet days together, Jack?"

There was a silence on the line. And a change of mood, she felt. She brought the receiver closer to her ear.

"Jack?"

"I'm here. When is Thanksgiving?"

"Not this Monday, but the next."

"I can find out, Maggie. I'll let you know."

In the car driving back to Sweetbarry, she thought how some nights in dreams she still put a hand to his face and kissed him on the lips. They were always so much younger in the dreams. So light and with so much unlived life before them, and viewed in this way, it was true that experience was not a gain, but a loss. A long time ago Manssourian had written that line on the blackboard as a topic for discussion.

She drove with the ocean blue and vast to her left. St. Margaret's Bay, Hubbards, East River, the detour through Gold River. The Martin's River bridge. The soft-sprung

Buick leaning into the turns. Hold on, Maggie, her father had liked to say to her. And grinned proudly. It's like racing a couch. But so much power when you need it. Want to see?

In places, fog had rolled in, then a mile later the view was clear again and the afternoon sun turned the ocean a dark blue with a band of turquoise on the horizon.

That night there was another storm. Not very bad, but bad enough to remind her it was time to board up the seaside window. There were fitted plywood sections in the boathouse, four of them for this purpose, and in the morning she dragged them out and hoisted them up by the handles and set them into the rests and spun the wing nuts. She could do only three boards before the wind picked up and the fourth board nearly carried her away like a sail. She dropped it and went in search of Franklin.

Already it was blowing so hard she had to hold on to trees and bushes as she walked. Then it began to rain.

An hour later the three of them in foul-weather gear had fixed the remaining window board, and now they were at work on the fall trusses. Franklin was in the house, up in the attic crawl space, and he reached out through the special hatches in the gable peaks and snapped the hooks into the eyes of the spine bolt that doubled the ridge beam from end to end. He dropped the steel cables to the ground, and she and Aileen shackled them and fed them out and hooked them into the four anchors cemented into rock a distance from the house.

Franklin came back down and then they set the levers into the turnbuckle frames and then watched Aileen, who stood leaning into the wind and rain, giving hand signals as they took turns putting tension into the opposing cables until they were tight enough to hum at the same frequency in the storm.

Over at Aileen's house they did the same, window boards and cables and turnbuckles, and before very long their little houses stood firm and square, snugged down with the wires humming. It was darker inside, but they were ready for the real weather that would be coming any day now.

Overnight it calmed and the rain stopped, but the next day brought more heavy clouds and high winds. Aileen was in her Vauxhall, in the pick-up lane at the Save-Easy, when she saw Danny's truck. Danny was behind the wheel, and a man in the passenger seat was busy wiping the mist off the window with his hands. She was about to get out and wave when she recognized the man. It was John Patrick Croft. They drove past as she waited for her groceries, and then the truck swung toward the exit and the brake lights flashed once and they were gone.

All the way home she drove gripping the steering wheel hard while the car was being battered by gusts of wind. In places where the wind came straight onshore, waves leapt so high she could see daylight through water thin and green like glass. Bits of seaweed rained down on the car.

She was upset about Danny still having anything to do with John Patrick, after all that had passed with the police and the boat. That night she lay listening for him to come home, and she could not sleep. At one time when she heard the screen door over at Margaret's, she got out of bed and put on a slicker and boots and a wool hat, and gripped the flashlight.

She called out to Margaret and then followed the yellow beam of her light among rocks and bushes.

"Is everything all right?" Margaret shouted.

"No, it's not!" she shouted back, and when she was near she said, "I saw Danny today, and guess who was in the truck with him."

"Who?"

"John Patrick Croft."

"Was he. Is that so bad?"

They stood holding on to trees, Margaret with the safety glasses on and the old baseball cap.

"Well, yes, it is bad," said Aileen. "After all that's happened with those criminals asking for him and the police cautions and all? Would you please talk to Danny once more? I don't want to go on harping at him, and he won't listen to me anyway. He'll listen to you before anyone else. Just one more time, Margaret."

"Talk to him and say what?"

"Something about finding someone other than John Patrick to help him. About the police. About not losing our boat. Common sense."

"I can try, Aileen. I'll think about it."

Twenty-Eight

BECAUSE OF THE WEATHER and the constant possibility of some sort of emergency, she no longer dressed up for work at her desk. Now it was usually an old wool skirt and a sweater under the jacket she'd found in the work room, and boots loosely laced to step into and out of.

In the morning after her office phone calls the storm had lessened, and she was in the forest again, tacking the last name signs to trees. On one of the white pines a large branch about fifteen feet up had cracked and was hanging down. She brought half the extension ladder and the handsaw, and wrangled the ladder up against the tree and climbed it. Not until she was up there did she realize that this was not something she should be doing, standing fifteen feet up on an unsteady ladder with no one holding it, sawing away at a branch.

Earlier, on the phone, Hugh had been testy, and he'd asked when she was finally coming back.

"I think you've been gone long enough, Margaret," he'd said. "I want you back in person here with us, okay? Attending meetings, answering your bloody phone, not a thousand miles away, but with your ass, if you'll pardon the expression, in your chair behind your desk. Is that clear? So when? I want a firm date."

"How about right after Thanksgiving, Hughie. It's only a week away."

"Don't *Hughie* me on this one. I want you back here."

"Okay. But just another week, Hugh. Please. I promise. Absolutely."

He'd grumbled a bit more, but in the end he'd agreed.

The saw kept binding and she had to pause often. Eventually the branch came off and crashed to the ground. Resin on her hands, scrapes, and a long sliver driven in just now from somewhere.

The branch was big, much bigger on the ground than it had looked up in the tree. She would have to drag it somewhere and chop it up, but she wasn't ready to deal with that now.

She put away the ladder and then sat for a while in her favourite spot on the rock shelf, with her eyes closed and salt air blowing into her face.

One reason she was in no hurry to fly back to Toronto was that she was making progress here. Inner progress. The previous day in this very spot she had fully accepted for the first time that what had happened with Andrew could never be undone. Never changed. Never. That the only thing she could ever hope to change was how she saw it. If she found a way.

She stood up and walked back to the house and showered. She used a needle and tweezers on the sliver, then rubbing alcohol and a Band-Aid.

When she came out of the bathroom, the phone rang. It was the inspector telling her they had found the missing boat, and a salvage operation was underway. He told her where it was and said that Sullivan was already there.

She ate a bite of lunch and then changed into her coat and street shoes and got into the Buick. She took the highway south and followed the turnoff to Rag Bay and then the two-track, and before long she saw the cars and the tractor and a boat trailer. She pulled over in the weeds and climbed out. The trailer was half submerged and they were winching a Cape Islander onto it, and as it came up and met the rollers, water gushed from a great hole low in the starboard bow and from another hole closer to the stern.

She stood next to Sully, watching, and nearby the same diver was leaning against his van, pulling off his wetsuit legs.

"A birdwatcher saw the top of the antenna mast sticking out at low tide," said Sully.

By mid-afternoon the boat was in Telford Herman's yard, and Sully had run police tape around the shed. Sorensen had arrived, and now he and Sully were up in the boat, inspecting it with hand lights. No one else was allowed in the shed.

"That's Fergie's boat," Telford said to her. "Pat Ferguson. The cops don't want to say, but we know. We been keeping his engine running. It's an old Volvo job. Cast iron. Lasts forever. Do you know him?"

"I do. When his wife was still alive I got my eggs from her. Good brown eggs."

"Mrs. Herman got them there too. When Helen passed he tried to keep the egg business going, but he didn't know the first thing about chickens or eggs. And he hasn't been fishing in years, not since the licences became so hard to get. But he knows the water and where the wildlife is and the diving spots, and so he takes tourists out for his upkeep. In the winters we hauled and stored his boat for free eggs and then for nothing."

Minutes later Sorensen came down the ladder.

"Any sign of him?" said Telford.

"Can't say. What would cause that damage?"

"Rocks. Wave action against rocks, if the boat got away.

I'd say it's been on the bottom for some time. Not just a few days. From all the mud and silt. Many tides washing through it."

"How long?" said Sorensen.

"Weeks."

"That could be. Is it fixable?"

"Probably. Cost a bit, but it's still a decent boat. A bit weird with that add-on cabin, but some people might like that. I'd have to take a closer look. But just so you know, I don't want it in my shed for too long because the shed makes money. We can get it out and up on a cradle in the back."

"No, we can't," said Sorensen. "I need to bring in forensics, and they'll take a very close look. We'll pay you the same day rate we paid for Danny's boat. You just call the office, Telford. For now the boat gets locked up and Sergeant Sullivan will post a guard."

She followed Sorensen to his car. Daylight was fading. He opened the trunk and sat on the chrome bumper while he pulled off the rubber boots and put his leather shoes back on and tied the laces. He looked weary to her.

"It's Pat Ferguson, isn't it?" she said. "Telford recognized the boat."

"Yes, it is. Do you know him?"

"Everybody knows him. He must have been on your list of right boats and right skills."

"Yes, he was on our list. We just couldn't find him. Or his boat."

"Maybe they took it and then got rid of it."

"I don't think so. They weren't sailors."

"Maybe they threatened him. Forced him to take them out."

"Possibly. Or promised him money."

He finished with his shoes and stood up.

"Forensics will find even the smallest remaining trace of what went on. Signs of struggle. Blood. Bullet holes. In the meantime we'll keep looking for him. But I think we all know what went on here."

"Do we?"

He reached for his boots, set them in the trunk and closed the lid hard. He turned around to look at her. "Do you know John Patrick Croft, Mrs. Bradley?"

"I do."

"Maybe go and talk to him. Tell him about today."

Twenty-Nine

NEXT MORNING AFTER her office phone calls she drove into the city. She parked at the harbour wall, where she could look out the windshield onto the water and the sailing ships that were in, among them the *Catalina* and the *Miss Elizabeth*. Crews were busy on decks, and on the *Miss Elizabeth* a man in a bosun's chair over the side was working with paint and brush.

She walked to the Trade Building and up the wooden stairway and along the hallway until she saw the brass sign for the Moynihan Charter Company. She knocked on the door and went in. The girl at the desk looked up and said, "Yes, ma'am?"

She handed the girl her business card and said she wanted to see Mr. Moynihan on an urgent matter.

The girl looked at the card. "Just a minute, ma'am." She rose and went into another room. Margaret heard voices and then Mr. Moynihan in a sports jacket and pressed trousers stood in his open door.

"Mrs. Bradley," he said. He looked at her and back at the card. "A lawyer. Please come in." He closed the door after her and asked her to sit.

"I'm not here as a lawyer, Mr. Moynihan. I am looking for John Patrick Croft. I know he's not working for you any more, but would you perhaps know where I can find him?"

"John Patrick." He rose and walked to the door and opened it. "Doreen, can you look up John Patrick in the Rolodex?"

He stood waiting. His office was carpeted and panelled. One wall was all naval charts on corkboards, another wall had ship's models mounted with small lights shining down on them. The window overlooked the harbour and the open sea beyond. Dark clouds racing, and spits of rain hard against the glass.

He came back with a piece of paper and handed it to her. "That's just up the hill from here. Can I ask what it is you want with him? He can be a bit of a wild card at times, but on the whole he's one of the best skippers I know. That thing in the harbour was unfortunate."

"What happened?"

"A near collision with a motorboat in the approach.

He was under sail and had the right of way but had to veer off sharply to avoid it. Some passengers took a tumble, and one woman hit her head on something." He shrugged. "It's possible he was carrying too much sail for the approach. Anyway, the insurance company . . . what can I say?"

"The insurance company told you to fire him?"

"Not in those words. They paid the woman's claim and they weren't happy."

"How is he getting by? Do you know? Has anyone else hired him?"

He was studying her now with his eyes narrowed. Taking his time. "I wouldn't know. Maybe he's freelancing, but I wouldn't know. You can ask him yourself when you see him."

She looked at the piece of paper in her hand. Then she stood up. "Thank you, Mr. Moynihan."

She had to knock three times, but somehow between the knocks she felt he was in. Then the door opened. It was the side entrance to a house, a basement apartment. He stood in jeans and grey wool socks and a denim shirt. A full head taller than she, black wavy hair, dark eyes. Taller and even more solid than Danny or Sullivan.

He blinked in the light, then he recognized her.

"Mrs. Bradley," he said. "I'm not usually home this time of day, but I was waiting for a call."

"This won't take long, John Patrick. You'll have heard of the two dead young people that were found at Crieff. And of the men who came to Aileen's house looking for you and Danny. One of them had a gun."

"Yes, I heard. Danny told me. And a police inspector came and showed me pictures and asked me questions."

"Pictures of the kids and of the suspects?"

"Yes."

"Did you know the men?"

He leaned back against the door frame now, looking at her. "What's this about?"

"Just a question. Did you know them?"

"I did. Would you like to come in? Or wait. Let me get my boots on and let's stand under the overhang."

His boots were on the landing, and he wiggled his sock feet into them and came outside.

"Just to get this out of the way," he said, "I had nothing to do with Crieff Island. Nothing."

"Then how did you know the suspects?"

He opened his mouth to say something, but then he closed it again.

"How, John Patrick? What did you tell the inspector?"

"I told him what happened. That they did approach me a few weeks ago to take them out on a run, but I told them I didn't have a boat. They'd heard that Danny was helping me out. Since I got fired. It's a small community and word gets round. I've been doing properties for him, in his boat. With the storms coming, he's behind."

"And when they approached you, what happened?"

"I said no."

"How much money were they offering?"

"At first three thousand, and when I said no they went up to four."

"Four thousand dollars. And you said no. Why?"

He stepped out from under the overhang and looked up into the drizzle. "I should go."

"Why did you say no, John Patrick? Because it's illegal?"

"Maybe. Or maybe because I didn't have a boat. As I kept telling them." He blushed like a boy, big solid man that he was, and she liked him for it.

"You mean if you'd had a boat, you might have done it? What if you got caught?"

"No one ever gets caught. And do you know how much money four thousand dollars is for one of us? For a couple of hours' work? In and out so fast?"

"Of course I know. I've spent half my life here. I was practically born here. So was my father."

"I know that. But you never had to depend on the local economy for your income. Nor your father, or AJ. But we do. I do. Danny does. And we know the currents and the tides, and we've had the charts in our heads since we been kids. To find our way in the dark out there all we need is a watch, a compass, and a pit log. Now with the fishing in such poor shape, that's our last best marketable skill for some of us, and with the new global positioning technology coming, we'll soon lose that too."

"Did you or Danny ever do a run for someone?"

"Don't be asking those questions now, Mrs. Bradley."

"But I'd like to know."

"Maybe you don't really, and maybe I don't want to say."

"Don't you."

"No."

"I ask because there is something else. Do you know old Fergie? Pat Ferguson?"

"Sure."

"Well, it turns out it was probably Fergie who did the run to Crieff. The truck the police found with the blood of that gunman in it was his, and now they've found his boat as well. With big holes in it, in twenty feet of water down in Rag Bay. The police are still searching for Fergie himself, but yesterday when I spoke to the inspector it didn't sound like he has much hope of finding him alive."

The drizzle had turned into rain now, and it came down soaking his shoulders and it came down on his head and face but he stood there unmoving, looking at her. Rainwater flattening his hair and running down his face and he not caring or perhaps not even noticing.

"Makes you think, doesn't it, John Patrick?"

He stirred. He looked up at the rain and back at her. "I should be gett'n inside."

But she couldn't let him go just yet. There was something else she wanted from him and now was the time.

"Wait," she said. "Please." She reached and pulled at his sleeve. "Step under here for another minute. There's one more thing. Something different. You knew my son, Andrew, didn't you?"

"Yes, of course I did. The aviator."

She had never heard anyone refer to her boy as *the aviator* and it touched her in a new way. Coming from this man there was so much in it. There was male pride in it, pride in the dangerous life, and respect for rank and accomplishment in the military world. And an echo of Michael's comments and of Jack's as well.

"I knew Andrew since we been boys," said John Patrick. "And the last few years we went out many times in Danny's boat, the three of us."

"Did you? I wasn't aware of that."

"No? In the summers, probably when you and your husband weren't out here. And last year, when they'd already signed him up. He wanted to learn about handling boats. I liked him."

"And was he learning?"

"Yes, he was. He had guts and quick instincts. I taught him about navigation, and he wanted to learn it even though he was joking that as a pilot he'd always have a navigator. I taught him about feeling the wind on his cheek and about seasonal currents and about the drifts raising up and shifting on our bars. I taught him about quartering to keep a course against tides and waves, which he said was a lot like crabbing an airplane. I taught him to find his way in a fog. In the pitch-dark. It's a different world out there in the dark, very different."

"I'm sure. And was he learning all that?"

She wanted to hear more, whatever it was. More about her boy from this man whom she felt sure Andrew had respected.

"Yes, he was learning. I was sorry when I heard, and sorry for your loss, Mrs. Bradley. I still am. But the other thing, that's how it happened, when those two men came around. The way I told you."

She stood looking at him, the two so close under the

overhang in the half-dark of the day and rain coming down hard and loud on the concrete walk.

"Does Mr. Moynihan have your phone number?"

"He should."

"If you're not sure then please write it down on a piece of paper and give it to me."

"Why?"

"Just do it."

He stepped inside and was gone for a minute. When he came back he handed her a slip of paper.

She took it and put it in her coat pocket. "Thank you for talking to me, John Patrick," she said. "And thanks for being honest. And for what you said about Andrew."

She nodded at him and then held both hands up over her head and walked away into the rain.

Fifteen minutes later she climbed the stairs to Moynihan's office again. He was standing by the girl's desk, and when she came in he looked up.

"Mrs. Bradley," he said. "So soon again. And you're all wet."

"Yes. Can I see you for a few more minutes?"

He waved her into his office. She took off her coat and hung it over a chair and when the door was closed she said, "I want to propose a contra deal. You rehire John Patrick

Croft and pay him what he's worth, I mean a good wage, and in exchange for that I'll give you two months of free legal services. Not exclusively, but a great deal of my attention. By telephone, telex, and courier."

He was clearly surprised at that. They were standing between his desk and the door, in the blended light from the window and the old-fashioned banker's lamp on his desk. In that light the ship's models on the wall behind him looked like beautiful and mysterious birds.

"Mrs. Bradley," he said, "I don't know what to say. But I'm listening. You should know that the tourist season is over. No more cruises this year. No more charters."

"So use him on some other ship."

"On some other ship. As though ships grew on trees."

"Don't they?"

"Only very small ones," he said with surprising humour. "I do have two deliveries. I bought a trawler in the States that I need to bring here, and I'm taking a cruiser down to South America. And there may be more."

"So use him for that. You said he is one of the best skippers you ever had and the mishap in the harbour wasn't really his fault. Rehiring him would also send an important signal to the rest of the shipping community."

"Yes, it would do that. How about three months of legal services?"

"No. Two months, Mr. Moynihan. Eight weeks. It's worth many thousands, and you'll be amazed at the things a good lawyer can set in motion and accomplish in eight weeks. Even part-time and on the phone and by courier."

He smiled at her. "And your firm will agree?"

"I'm sure they will. I'll sell it to the partners as a pro bono opportunity to move into the maritime business. Some of it will be on my own time."

"I see. But do you know anything about the legal aspects of operating and buying and selling ships, Mrs. Bradley?"

"No. Not yet. But I do know about buying and selling multi-million-dollar businesses and real estate. Liability laws. International third-party property transactions. Tax jurisdictions and tax advantages and tax deferral. How different could ships be? In law it's all about the intent and the fabric of the law. From there you go to the threads and how they interweave. Everything connects in important ways with everything else. I'm a quick study, Mr. Moynihan."

"Yes, I imagine you are." He waved a hand at his desk and the chairs. "Shall we sit?"

Thirty

BACK IN SWEETBARRY she went up to Andrew's room again. She opened the window and took off the sheets the parents had slept on and put them in the washing machine. Then she put a fresh set of sheets on the bed. She carried the lead bucket back into the room and put it down in its corner and finally went to fetch the driftwood chair as well. She sat down on it.

She did not know how the parents were doing it. She could see the result, but the means of it were to her unidentifiable. The how. The one single image of them that had stayed with her the most had been of the two in the back seat of the car, sitting so close together, being so close that no daylight could get between them. Could separate them. It had made her want to step on the brake and pull over and really look at this and take it in. It had made her feel ashamed.

She shifted in the chair and looked around.

The Mother's Cross. How aptly named. She would not be changing anything in this room just yet. If ever. How could she, and what would be the point?

A black Ford pickup truck pulled up on her rock, and John Patrick climbed out and walked up to her house. She could see him through her kitchen window, taking off his cap and running his hand through his hair and standing for a moment to collect himself before he knocked on her door.

"I came to thank you," he said the moment she'd opened up. "Mr. Moynihan called me and I've just been to see him. Thank you so much."

They shook hands, and then she beckoned and he bent down and she gave him a hug. Big man that he was, big shoulders on him.

She remained in the open door while he turned away and walked to his truck, climbed up and rolled down the window and grinned at her. He drove off and turned left onto Aileen's rock and blew his horn.

The door opened and Danny came down the stoop, in his jeans worn through at the knees like Andrew's had been out here, and running shoes and a lined work shirt with snap buttons. So eager to be men accepted by other men, they were. To be seen as strong and sure in this world, which would sniff out any weakness in an instant and move in.

They stood and talked. John Patrick pointed more than once in the direction of her house, and she watched them for a while through the trees and across the rocks.

It was getting dark and the air was still and heavy. She could feel it deep inside her ears. Clouds were boiling, black and purple towers of great height like an underworld event.

An hour later the storm made landfall. There was a long moment of absolute stillness in the air, a vacuum in which nothing moved, no leaf stirred and no bird flew. For that moment she felt dizzy, and she left the kitchen and crossed to the living room to sit in a solid chair, and halfway there had to embrace the king post for support. There was a shock wave and a sound like an express train passing, and she felt the entire house rise up against the cables and tremble and hang there for moments before it settled back down onto the foundation blocks. The lights went out and the steel cables sang and the house frame and all the woodwork picked up the vibration, and the entire house hummed and moaned. Out the kitchen window she could see that the power line had come down, and for a few seconds the wire was spitting sparks and dancing like a snake. Then it lay still.

There was a strange dark-yellow light out there in which sea spray and leaves sailed far inland, and through the walls she could hear trees crashing in her forest. A large branch smashed through the window in the hallway and hung there while water poured in and spread quickly.

She lit a coal-oil lamp from AJ's time and went to work with mop and bucket. Two hours later, during a brief lull in the storm, she put on the coverall and boots and heavy gloves and went outside and wrestled the branch back out. It looked like the one she'd cut off from the white pine and left on the ground.

She would have liked to call Aileen but the telephone was out as well, and it was still blowing too hard to walk over. And so she used their old signalling device, which was an iron rod and a dangling piece of rail, and when Aileen came out of her house and stood on the stoop they waved to each other in a flagless semaphore that everything was all right.

She crawled under the house to check on the braided flex-hose plumbing connections, and another hour or two later she made it to the boathouse and found the piece of fitted plywood that she should have put over the hallway window but forgot. She dragged it to the house and put it up now, and then back inside mopped up more water and swept up glass.

She took a shower with what she feared might well be the last hot water for a while, and then put on her nightgown and housecoat and slippers. High up at the back of a kitchen cupboard there was an old camp stove and a bottle of emergency coal oil, and she stood on a chair to bring them down. She filled the tank and pumped in air for pressure, opened the valve, and put a match to the burner. It worked. She talked to it. Good little cooker, she said to it. Still working well. Good for you.

She opened a tin of ravioli and scraped that into a saucepan and set it on the stove and stirred. When it was bubbling, she poured it into the blue cereal bowl and set the coal-oil lamp on the table in front of her.

Thank you, she said to the lamp and the little stove and the very house sheltering her, and began to eat.

—

In the morning there was still no electricity, and she boiled her coffee water on the camp stove and poured it through the hand filter into the Thermos. The fridge was still cold inside, but it would not be so for much longer. Then in her slicker and boots she walked down to inspect her forest.

It had suffered badly. Trees had been uprooted and broken, remnants standing to heights beyond reach and long white scars running down where bark had been peeled. Root balls six feet across had been levered up from the soil put there by her father's eighty-eight trucks, soil settled for three generations but not a hundred, and the root system not deep enough to withstand yesterday's onslaught.

It took that day and part of the next before the road into town and the shore road were cleared by workers with chainsaws, and on the way to Telford Herman's boatyard she drove past several repair crews mending power lines. But at the yard itself there was hardly any damage. Telford said it had to do with the way the coastline curved where they were and gave them shelter. Like a natural harbour, he said. They were lucky that way.

She explained about her forest, and Telford and his son stood and listened.

"Quite a few tamaracks down in there," she said. "And white pines and Norway pines. And hardwoods too."

When she made her offer, they listened and nodded and talked about it. Then they all climbed into the Buick and drove there. They studied her forest and then they walked it, estimating the cost of the cleanup against the value of salvageable wood.

In the end she and Telford shook hands, and the next day they came with horses and flatbed carriages and a crew with chains and hydraulic gear and a tractor winch. It took three days, and when all the logs and root balls had been hauled away and the ground more or less levelled, her forest was much thinned, thinned by one-quarter perhaps.

"But look on the bright side, Margaret," said Telford. "It needed a bit of clearing anyway, and you might never have had the heart to do it."

From the house she could now see the ocean through the trees. She could see daylight on the ground, and at night she'd be able to walk it without safety glasses. And on a clear day there would be sunlight where there hadn't been any in years. Forest flowers might grow, new seeds take root.

In the morning the telephone was still down, as was the power, but around noon a uniformed postal clerk on a bicycle brought her a telegram. She ripped it open. It said,

COMING OUT FOR THANKSGIVING—STOP—
CP AIR 2:15 PM HALIFAX FRIDAY—JACK.

She gave the postie a generous tip and hurried over the rock to tell Aileen.

The power and the telephone came back on that evening. Her refrigerator hummed obligingly and the red pilot light on the water heater glowed.

She slept well that night, and in the morning she luxuriated in a hot shower and washed her hair and blow-dried it. She put on makeup and then stood in front of her open closet and chose her clothes for the day. She spent three hours at her desk and after lunch got into the Buick and drove north along the coast to pick him up at the airport.

In the evening they had dinner at the Outrigger. They were careful with words, careful even looking at each other. Tammy had picked that up as soon as she'd seen them, and she was extra-attentive. She showed them to a good table by a waterside window. Strings of electric lights shone on fishing boats and on the dock planking and on old bollards worn down and polished by hawsers for years.

"I'll get you a drink on the house," Tammy said. "And then I'll come and take your orders. Wasn't that blow something?"

That night in dreams she was in Beechwood Cemetery in Ottawa, standing by Andrew's headstone with the black cross and his unit insignia and his name on it. A white stone, one among so many in vanishing lines this way and that. So very many of them, in such silence, such enormous peace and so much fine company. She kissed her fingers and put them to his stone, and at the touch she woke and saw the pale square window and Jack asleep on the other side of the bed.

Part of her house had yet to dry out, and to help it along she kept the cookstove going, and the fireplace, and she opened all the windows wide. Because of that, Aileen said she would host the annual Thanksgiving dinner at her house, even though it wasn't her turn.

The plan for dinner was turkey and Brussels sprouts and yellow beans and squash and mashed potatoes, all fresh from the Annapolis Valley, and a pumpkin pie with blueberries and whipped cream for dessert.

While Margaret and Aileen were busy in the kitchen,

Jack and Danny worked at replacing her window and patching plaster. Franklin strained the new blueberry wine through a filter.

As was often the case a few days after a storm, the sky had cleared and the weather was beautiful. Sunny and cold and no wind at all. Flaming leaves adrift and cold water lapping on cold, smooth stone. A chance of flurries in the forecast.

At one time she and Aileen were up in the blueberries, picking the last of them for the dessert. Once in a while they stood and straightened their backs, and they ate a sweet berry or two, looking down at the rocks and trees, at their wooden houses and the ocean, everything swept clean and sparkling, and far out, nearly at the horizon, the white shape of a large sailing ship.

In the late afternoon she and Jack began dressing for dinner. The Thanksgiving get-togethers were the one event in the year they had all agreed to dress up for, just to make a difference. She'd wear the dark green dress, and Aileen would probably be wearing a tartan skirt with a blouse and her black cashmere cardigan with the silver thistle pin from her grandmother.

At one point, when Margaret came out of the bathroom with her head cocked, struggling with an earring, she saw

Jack sitting on the side of the bed like a man lost, with his hands on his trouser knees the way she'd seen another father sit not long ago.

Since his arrival they had not once spoken about Andrew, even though it was always as if their boy were in the room with them. They hadn't spoken much at all, but then not much could be said, nor were any new thoughts ready to be committed to words.

But now, when she saw him sitting like that, something welled up in her and she put the earring on the dresser and walked over to the bed and sat down next to him. She put her arm in his and sat very close. And after a while she moved closer still.

They sat like this for minutes while the orange sunspot from the window moved across the floor, from the hardwood onto the edge of the carpet. From over on the other rock they could hear Aileen calling for Danny, and Danny answering. They could hear seabirds and the wind and the ocean. And once or twice in those minutes she reached up and with the fingertips of her free hand wiped her eyes.

Thirty-One

TWO WEEKS BEFORE CHRISTMAS she was on an airplane back to Paris. Thérèse was launching a book—perhaps her last, she'd said, one never knew—and Margaret was able to combine the event with an important client visit that Hugh wanted her to make. Jack was in Sweden, and he might be able to join her in time, or he might not. They had once again recognized and accepted that about each other, that his work rescued him as much as hers did her.

In Toronto she had moved back into the main house. Jack tried to be home more often, and she tried not to put in such long hours. It worked some of the time. When they were both home they had candlelit dinners, not at the long table but at the smaller pinewood table by the window.

Most important, they were beginning to be able to smile at each other again. To smile and to talk, because words were beginning to lose their danger.

She still dreamt about Andrew, and at times she saw him in fleeting day visions, and she hoped she always would. Once from a streetcar she saw him raking leaves in a city park, and one night coming home in a taxi she saw him in a passing car.

Sweetheart, she said to him, and turned to watch his lights recede.

For some reason, tonight she did not mind being on this airplane. Perhaps because it was an overnight flight and it was half empty. Calm and not so bright. It had left Toronto in the evening and would be in Paris in the morning. Now the movie had finished and the lights were turned low. She eased up the window blind and looked out. A quarter moon and a bright star nearby. Their reflections on the long metal of the airplane wing.

She thought back to the first time she met Thérèse at the school, to the Women's Stories sessions in the lounge. To their last talk under palm trees at the residence. She was beginning to believe that what Thérèse had said that night about loss might in fact be possible; that her sorrow and the way she might learn to live with it would in time become something like a friend. In good moments such as now, she could see the shape of thoughts and emotions that might permit it.

If so, it would probably happen in the cottage in Toronto. Some evenings and weekends when Jack was away, she still walked down there to spend quiet time in the kitchen, since that was where for some reason she could connect most easily with the boy. The corner with the padded bench and the table was where he came to meet her. Where they could sit and communicate without words now, just the two of them. She knew it was all just imag-inings in her heart, but in some way it was also real, and slowly, slowly in this way she might be able to let him go.

She reclined the seat a bit and pulled up the blanket. Tucked it in around her chin and closed her eyes. A deep breath in and out.

Thank you, she said.

ACKNOWLEDGEMENTS

For all their support with *The Hour of the Fox* I wish to thank the team at McClelland & Stewart led by Jared Bland, publisher, and Kelly Joseph, publishing manager, and including Erin Kelly, Scott Loomer, Max Arambulo, Bonnie Maitland, Ashley Dunn, Kimberlee Hesas, Rachel Cooper, Valentina Capuani, and Terra Page. My thanks also go out to Lara Hinchberger, my editor, to Ellen Levine my agent, and to you, Heather, always my first reader.

ABOUT THE AUTHOR

The Hour of the Fox is KURT PALKA's seventh novel. His previous work includes *Clara*, which was published in hardcover as *Patient Number 7* and was a finalist for the Hammett Prize, and *The Piano Maker*, a national bestseller. Kurt Palka lives near Toronto.